# PERHAPS SHE'LL DIE

Also by
M. K. Preston

*Song of the Bones*

# PERHAPS SHE'LL DIE

by

M. K. PRESTON

INTRIGUE PRESS | DENVER

Published by: Intrigue Press, PO Box 102004, Denver, CO 80210
An imprint of Corvus Publishing



ISBN: 1-890768-58-8
First Intrigue Press Hardcover Edition / June 2001
Printed and bound in Canada

This book is a work of fiction. Names, characters, places and incidents are either the product of the author's imagination or are used fictitiously. Any resemblance to actual events or locales or persons, living or dead, is entirely coincidental. Although the author and publisher have made every effort to ensure the accuracy and completeness of information contained in this book, we assume no responsibility for errors, inaccuracies, omissions, or any inconsistency herein. Any slights of people, places or organizations are unintentional.

Designed by Magpie Creative Design

The Library of Congress has cataloged the hardcover edition as follows:
Preston, M. K., 1944-
Perhaps She'll Die: A Chantalene Mystery/by M. K. Preston.
p. cm.
ISBN 1-890768-33-2 (the hardcover edition)
1. Women Detectives--Oklahoma--Fiction.
2. Oklahoma--Fiction. I. Title.
PS3566.R4123 P4 2001
813'.6--dc21

00-054150

10 9 8 7 6 5 4 3 2 1

For my mother, who didn't live to see it published;
and for my husband, who did.

I am indebted to the Gadflies writers' group
for their valuable advice and encouragement,
and to mystery writer Carolyn Wheat for
showing me exactly what I needed to learn.

# PROLOGUE

Awakened by Socko's furious barking, Chantalene lay rigid in the darkness, listening.

Heavy footsteps shook the wooden floor of the old farmhouse. She heard a quick shout from her father, a muffled *thud,* then silence.

*What was happening out there?*

She pictured Daddy lying on the sofa minutes ago—*or was it hours?*—when she'd kissed him goodnight, the dark stubble of his beard scratchy against her cheek, his smell pleasant and boozy from celebrating the end of the trial. She'd been angry when Mama wouldn't let her attend—she was twelve, after all, old enough to know what a rape trial was about. But all was forgiven in her relief at Daddy's acquittal.

Heart pounding, she sat up in her bed and strained to hear.

Mama's voice—frantic, questioning. A heavy *thump* shook the living room wall and Socko snarled. Footsteps scraped out the front door, down the porch steps.

Then there was silence. Nothing left but Socko's frenzied barking.

Chantalene couldn't breathe. She threw her legs over the side of the bed and crept to the door of her bedroom. Pressing her ear to the door, she heard only the surging of her own heart.

*Was she alone? Where were Mama and Daddy?*

She turned the knob slowly, still holding her breath, and inched the door open.

Through the crack she saw Mama crouched in the darkness of the hallway, wildly digging through the closet. Chantalene opened her mouth to call out but stopped when she heard the choked hum of her mother's breathing, quick and desperate like an injured dog. Mama found something—Daddy's hunting knife?—then grabbed her coat and pulled it on over her nightgown.

When her mother turned, Chantalene closed the door quickly and scrambled back in bed, as if she'd been caught doing something wrong. She didn't know why; she only knew Mama wouldn't want her awake. Pulling the sheet up to her chin, she lay trembling, waiting.

She could feel Mama stop at her door, listening. Then Mama let Socko into the house and commanded him to hush and stay. Socko obeyed. Mama was agile and quick-tempered, a descendant of gypsies. When she was riled, nobody in the family—human or animal—crossed her. The front door closed and Mama's quick footsteps descended the porch steps.

Chantalene waited only a moment, but it seemed like forever.

Socko met her when she slipped out of her room. The big shepherd whined and pressed his body against her leg. She hurried to the front window and looked out.

The tail of Mama's long gown below her coat glowed white in the moonlight, bobbing across the wheat field.

Daddy was gone.

Chantalene grabbed her coat and shoes and looked for the shotgun. It, too, was gone. Nausea rolled through her stomach.

Quickly she stepped onto the front porch and shut

Socko inside the house, which set him barking again. Shoving her arms into the coat sleeves, she watched her mother cross through the barbed wire fence into the neighbor's pasture. Chantalene stuck bare feet into her cold loafers and followed.

October wind cut through her clothes. Mama was moving fast. Chantalene slipped quickly between the fence wires and ran to close the distance between them, careful to stay far enough behind that her mother wouldn't hear and send her back to the house.

Far ahead of them, glimmers of light like flashlight beams jerked a path across the pasture, toward an old haybarn that squatted dark and silent in the moonlight. Half a mile from any farmhouse, the barn was hidden from the road by the rise of the land. As she drew closer, a gleam of light shone through cracks in the wooden siding of the barn, as if someone was inside, waiting.

*Why would they take him there?* It must have something to do with the trial. Fear stitched her breathing as the flashlights disappeared into the barn. *What would they do to him?*

When her mother reached the barn, Chantalene crept close enough to see and hid in the tall grass. A startled grasshopper ticked up and flew away. She clamped her mouth shut to stop the ragged sound of her breath in the stillness.

Mama didn't go to the door where the flashlights had entered, but circled around to the side. Then, as Chantalene watched, time slipped into slow motion: Mama threw off her coat and scaled the side of the barn like a cat, clinging to knotholes and cracks with her bare feet and hands.

A high-pitched whine rose in Chantalene's throat. Her mother pulled herself through a window into the hayloft and disappeared.

Hunched in the timothy and buffalo grass, the girl waited, trembling. Should she follow?

Glimmers of light seeped through the cracks, and she heard someone yell but the wind blew the sound away.

She stood up and started toward the barn.

A scream—more animal than human—skewered her where she stood, silencing all the sounds of the night. Only when the wail stopped did she recognize the voice as her mother's.

For a moment even the wind held its breath. Her skin stood up in crawling ridges; the echo rang in her ears. And across the stillness she heard her mother shrieking—an old Gypsy curse, her voice wild and horrible. A promise of gruesome death to all present, and to their children.

The power and rage of that voice electrified her. *Mama needed help!* Chantalene sprinted toward the barn.

Suddenly the door swung open. She dropped flat, hiding in the tall grass. Four hooded figures emerged from the barn and hurried into the shadows toward the road. Her mother wasn't with them, nor her father. She waited. In a moment a pickup engine started, then another. Maybe a third, she wasn't sure. The vehicles roared away, their tires grinding on the shale road.

She ran to the barn and slipped through the door.

Without moonlight, darkness swallowed the interior of the barn. She stopped, hugging her shaking body, and searched the shadows.

Framed against the cavernous dark in the center of the barn, a glowing apparition danced above the floor. Her mother's nightgown. A scream caught in her chest. Then she made out the shape of her father's body, a sagging mass, and her mother pressed against him, struggling to hold him while she reached with one arm toward the noose that pulled up on his neck.

For a moment, Chantalene thought they were suspended there together, hanging from the taut rope. Then she recognized the dark, blocky shapes of hay bales stacked up beneath their feet. Something glinted in her mother's outstretched hand; she was trying to cut the rope.

Chantalene scrambled onto the bales, the dry straw piercing her palms and knees. Struggling to stand, she braced her feet and held her father's slack body in both arms, pressing her face against his stomach. She couldn't see his face, didn't want to see. She smelled her mother's sweat and rage as she sawed the rope, the awful hum rising in her throat like a thousand angry bees.

The rope gave. Her father's weight dropped like a stone, toppling the hay bales, knocking all three of them to the dirt floor. The dead weight of him pinned her to the earth.

He was so *heavy,* limber as bagged water. Could this be her daddy? For the rest of her life, she would strain under that weight ... .

It took both of them to roll him off. When Chantalene opened her eyes again, her father's face stared at her, distorted and dark, eyes open in terror.

She jerked her head away, a strangled cry escaping her throat. Mama clutched her, and they lay trembling in each other's arms on the loamy-smelling floor of the barn, gasping for breath. She was too scared to cry.

Her mother's hoarse voice scraped like paper in the darkness. "He's dead." And then, "Did they see you?"

"No."

*"Are you sure?"*

"Yes."

"Thank God. *Don't tell anyone! Never tell anyone what you saw!"*

"I won't, Mama."

They lay still, listening to the wind moan through the barn, straining for the sound of returning footsteps. Wind rustled outside the barn and groaned through rafters. An owl mourned from the elms.

"Will they kill us, too?"

"No, baby. I won't let them." Mama held her tighter. "We'll go back to the house, get the truck." Her voice struggled for calm. "We'll run away."

"What about Daddy?"

Mama stroked her hair. "We have to leave him here," she said. Her voice left no room for argument. "We can't help him now. We have to save ourselves."

Holding hands, they stumbled through the pasture toward home, running through an ocean of grass. Mama's bare feet were bleeding.

Their house looked eerie and small in the moonlight. Socko's barking reverberated from inside. He burst out the door when Mama dragged her inside and down the hall.

"Here's a pillowcase. Take only what you can fit inside. Hurry!"

They didn't turn on the lights. Frantic now, as if pursued, Chantalene ran to her bedroom and dressed quickly in warm clothes. She stuffed jeans and a sweatshirt into her sack, and as she ran to get her toothbrush, heard the drone of a vehicle bouncing up the long driveway.

Mama heard it, too. They met in the hallway and clung to each other. Nowhere to hide! A blaze of light reflected on the wall and something hit the roof, then rolled off. Together they crept to the front window and saw a second torch arch through the darkness, this time onto the roof of the shed. A dark figure ran back to a light-colored pickup and it spun away.

The shed was afire and the truck was inside. Mama ran to the kitchen and snatched the keys. "Bring our sacks. Run!" she yelled, and was out the door. Chantalene ran—the pillowcases slung over her shoulder.

Chickens screamed and flapped into the night. The shed roof was blazing, driven by the wind, when they crawled into the truck and Mama turned the key.

"Mama! What about Socko?"

"He's on his own!"

The engine ground and stopped. A wail rose in Chantalene's throat. Smoke seared her lungs. Any moment the roof would collapse and burn them alive. The engine ground again, and again. Mama cursed the truck, hammered her fist on the steering wheel, and on the next try the motor caught and roared. She slammed the truck in gear and they shot forward, crashing through the flimsy wooden door of the shed in a blizzard of splinters and dust.

The tires churned gravel and they careened away. Looking back, Chantalene saw the shed cave inward, red-orange flames shooting into the night. The house had composition shingles; it hadn't caught fire. Socko stood in the yard, barking.

They lurched down the bumpy quarter-mile driveway. Mama raved and ranted, most of it making no sense. But Chantalene understood one sentence clearly. "They'll hunt me down, and if you're with me, they'll kill you, too!"

At the first corner, her mother wrenched the wheel and the truck fish-tailed in the loose shale. She was heading west, toward the Jenkses' house.

*"Don't ever tell anyone what you saw,"* Mama said again, and a fear worse than any she'd had that night froze Chantalene's throat. *Mama was going to leave her behind.*

Despite her begging, Mama left her with the only neighbor she trusted, and promised to come back.

She never saw her mother again.

# ONE

Parked along both shoulders of the dusty red road, pick-ups and battered farm trucks ticked in the rising heat. Chantalene rode her horse down the narrow corridor, her hand moving again to touch the letter folded into her jeans pocket. Oklahoma sun lasered perspiration from her red t-shirt.

The letter had appeared in her rural mailbox on Saturday, as innocently as news of a bake sale at the Baptist church or the tax liens against her land. She'd had forty-eight hours to plan this confrontation with her neighbors. The two days seemed as long as the twelve years she'd waited for such an opportunity.

She recognized Monkey Jenks' blue Ford pickup beside the road, and her shoulders tensed. And there was Willie Bond's shiny new stretch-cab, overburdened with chrome. Judging from the long line of vehicles, everybody in Tetumka was here. She had counted on that. Ever since she'd abandoned college and returned to this god-forsaken place six months ago, they'd treated her with suspicion. They knew why she'd come back. But they didn't know what was in the letter. She was their worst nightmare: an unforgiving messenger of the truth.

She urged the gray gelding across a shallow grader ditch, dismounted, and looped his reins around a fencepost. Whippoorwill pricked his ears forward, questioning.

"Not long, Whip, I promise." She patted his sleek neck.

By mid-September the first cool front should have thundered down from the northwest to signal the start of autumn. Instead, the distant Black Fork Mountains lay crackling in leftover August heat. Even the weather was behind the times in Tetumka. Despite a punishing sun, though, believers and non-believers alike had gathered this morning at Grant Selby's farm to watch Slim Jenks, Monkey's brother, witch for water.

Ducking between strands of barbed wire fencing, Chantalene followed the sound of voices. Her mouth tasted like dust when she approached the crowd gathered in a small field close to the Selby farmhouse. She lifted her chin and surveyed the scene.

Grant Selby and his wife had been getting by for thirty years with a windmill that pumped water a quarter mile to a supply tank behind the house. Now he'd decided if he could find water closer to the home site, he'd put in an electric pump and join the twentieth century before it passed into history. Finding a new well wasn't as crucial as if the Selbys had no water, so the event had taken on a festive atmosphere—Tetumka's version of a social occasion. As she approached, Chantalene heard bets being laid and covered, accompanied by laughter.

All the levity stopped when they saw her.

She took perverse pleasure in the way her presence struck the good folks of Tetumka silent. Even so, their hostile gaze made her uncomfortable, and her anger grew.

*Not yet,* she told them silently. *I'll choose my own moment.*

Avoiding their eyes, she scanned the ragged circle of onlookers. In the center, big Slim Jenks squatted with his back to her, talking to Grant Selby while he made adjustments on a forked willow stick with his pocketknife. She spotted Monkey on the perimeter of the circle and went to stand beside him.

Monkey and his wife Martha, who had tried their best to be foster parents to her, were among the few who'd speak to her in public since she'd moved back. And that might change after today. She felt a twinge of guilt, knowing how strongly the Jenkses would disapprove of what she was about to do.

She caught the glares of Big Willie and Opal Bond and their banty-rooster son, Little Willie. Her jaw tightened. Even the Reverend Graves was here, the "new" Southern Baptist minister who'd come to invite her to church when she'd first moved into her parents' old house, before his congregation warned him away. He'd lived here only five years and hadn't known her history, so they probably forgave him. She could picture his flock fleeing out the doors if she did show up in his church.

The children—what few were left in the aging community—would be attending the consolidated school near El Rio today. She was glad they weren't here.

Chantalene saw Monkey's eyes flick toward her as she approached. If he regretted her presence, he'd never show it. He tipped his stained hat and offered her a half-smile.

"Mornin', Chantalene."

"Hi, Monkey."

The men standing near Monkey receded half a step but were too curious to move away. None of them spoke.

"Didn't Martha come?" she asked.

With a nod of his head, Monkey indicated a cluster of women on the opposite margin of the circle. Martha Jenks stood nearly a head taller than her companions, Mrs. Selby and Thelma Patterson. Thelma was the postmistress, plump and friendly, an inveterate gossip. She must have closed the post office window this morning so she could attend. In a larger town, such a breach might get her fired, but even Uncle Sam was oblivious to what went on in Tetumka.

Thelma spotted Chantalene and waved, too gregarious to snub anyone, regardless of stigma. She nudged Martha, who also waved and motioned for Chantalene to cross over and join her. Mrs. Selby stiffened her neck.

Chantalene pretended not to read the gesture. She felt more comfortable with Monkey's amiable silences than with Martha's mothering. Just then Slim Jenks unfolded his lanky frame and pocketed his knife. All eyes focused on him, and Chantalene was saved the dishonor of refusing to stand with the womenfolk.

The farmers shuffled their feet in anticipation of the main event, and Chantalene waited, swallowing the dryness in her throat, her hand touching the letter in her pocket.

Slim Jenks was a curious figure, even in Opalata County. Quiet and reclusive, he lived alone on an isolated spread at the foot of the Black Forks. His land was pasture and woods, suited for cattle instead of farming. According to Martha, Slim could saw a mean fiddle and used to play for square dances years ago when Tetumka had a social life. Rumor had it he owned a rare violin and kept it in a case under his bed.

Slim also believed in the divining rod, and no one saw fit to discredit his belief, maybe because Slim stood six-foot-four without his boots and had once lifted the front end of a tractor to free a trapped neighbor. But that was in his youth, and Chantalene hadn't seen him since moving back, nor for several years before that while she was away at college.

Slim didn't look well. Always slender, today he reminded her of barbed wire, his bones poking up like tent poles under his clothes. His hair had gone gray and the sockets around his eyes looked sunken and dark. The contrast between her memory of him and the ghost she saw before her was shocking. What could be eroding Slim away like that? Cancer?

Finally, Grant Selby and Slim shook hands and Grant stepped back into the circle, which widened and left Slim alone in the center. Slim squinted into the sun—he was the only hatless man present—and gripped the forks of his divining rod in oversized hands. All voices fell silent, and Slim began a solemn stride across the acreage.

A peculiar prickle threaded Chantalene's backbone. She'd never actually witnessed a water witching, but somehow it felt—*familiar.* Her mother had witched the well on their home place, before she was born. For a moment, seduced by the strange ritual, she ignored the crinkle of the envelope in her pocket and the reason she'd come.

Slim's eyes never left the straight stalk of the willow branch, which pointed directly in front of him, parallel to the ground. The farmers watched it, too, even the doubters struck silent by Slim's determined steps. Back and forth he paced under the cloudless sky, patiently, never varying his gait.

When it happened, Chantalene felt the collective gasp around the circle. The tip of the willow rod quivered, then shook, then arched indisputably toward the earth. Everyone looked at Slim's big hands and saw his knuckles turn white on the forked stick, as if he were trying to hold the rod straight against some mysterious force that attracted it downward.

Chantalene's palms tingled. *She had known before it happened.* Deep beneath her breastbone, she had felt the pull of the willow rod, the hypnotic attraction between the wood and the water deep inside the earth. Her breath shortened, her fists clenching and unclenching at her sides.

God, it was hot out here.

She watched Slim's eyes: blue-gray as steel, betraying no emotion. When the tip of the rod pointed straight down, he stopped, crouched, and pulled from his hip pocket a small wooden stake, which he forced into the earth.

Chantalene exhaled. The farmers shifted from one leg to the other. They took off their hats and ran rough hands over their heads and set their hats on again. Streams of tobacco juice raised dust where they spackled the ground. She fidgeted, impatient, but the time wasn't right.

Without a word, Slim rose and walked to the opposite side of the acreage. There he started again, holding the willow fork firmly, the point parallel to the ground. Slowly he paced toward the upright stake, repeating exactly the motions he had gone through before, coming upon the staked spot from a different direction. As he drew closer, Chantalene held her breath, knowing what he knew, but Slim worked as objectively as a machine.

Just before he reached the marked spot, the willow stick began to vibrate. Within two feet of the stake, the rod swung downward until it was perpendicular to the ground. Again Slim stopped, produced a second marker, and inserted it a few feet away from the first. One more stake remained in his pocket.

A mumble passed through the crowd. Slim straightened and pulled out a red bandanna. He mopped his brow, his gaze lifting from his work for a moment. And that's when he saw her.

Chantalene was feeling wired, her eyes wide, lips parted. When Slim's flinty gaze met hers, she saw the color drain from his face, his mouth go slack. He froze, then his knees began to tremble. She felt the company of farm folk trace

Slim's gaze to her own, but she was astonished, unable to look away.

The willow stick slipped from his hand.

Beside her, Monkey moved quickly. He reached Slim just before his legs gave out and clamped a firm hand under his brother's elbow. Monkey led Slim away from the crowd to the shade of a blackjack tree.

Sweat trickled down Chantalene's neck. She had no idea what had just happened to Slim, but the accusing eyes of her neighbors reminded her why she'd come.

*Now. Do it now. Show the guilty bastards.*

She stepped to the center of the circle and picked up the divining rod.

Instantly the mumbling of the crowd ceased. With all eyes watching, she grasped the forks of the stick in sweating palms and began a measured tread across the plot from a third direction.

As she approached the two wooden spikes, the rod quivered in her hands—as she'd known it would. She kept walking, one deliberate step after another. The vibration grew and she strained to hold the branch straight. Then the point of the rod arched like a snake's neck, and her breath caught as the stick pulled toward the earth not three feet from Slim's two markers.

She jabbed the tip of the willow branch into the grass, forming a crooked triangle with the other markers. The split divining rod sprouted up from the earth like a forked tongue.

Straightening, her heartbeat pelting like rain, she hid shaking hands in her pockets. "There's your well, Mr. Selby," she said distinctly. "Looks like a good one."

She could have heard a cowchip drop in that field.

"Now that I have your attention, there's something I want you to know." She pulled the wrinkled envelope from her jeans. “Sheriff Justin sent me this copy of a letter he received last week from the warden at McAlester State Penitentiary. Seems a fellow on death row there wanted to clear his conscience and confess his sins.”

She cleared her throat and raised her voice, acutely aware of the stone-faced expressions surrounding her, especially Martha Jenks, whose eyes implored her to shut up.

“Among the crimes the convict admitted—without prompting—was the rape of a retarded girl near Tetumka twelve years ago.” She paused. “When you hanged my father, you murdered an innocent man.”

She drew a deep breath. *“And I know who you are.”*

# TWO

Chantalene expected at least a guilty murmur from the crowd after her pronouncement, but the faces circling her were silent as a tumor. Sweating, she turned and strode out of the circle. The good citizens parted to leave her a path. She felt their disapproving eyes while she mounted Whippoorwill and rode away.

It was a lie, of course.

She didn't know who'd killed her father—couldn't even remember the days surrounding his death. All she had left were grotesque nightmares that finally had driven her back to this isolated community, which was separated from the world not only by geography but by choice. The letter from McAlester had empowered her, at last, to shake the village tree and see what fell out.

This night, too, would be haunted.

*From the window of her bedroom, Chantalene saw Mama's resolute gait toward the chicken house, the chicken hook in her toughened hand. Daddy had made the long hook of heavy galvanized wire, with five inches on one end turned back in a sharp, narrow curve. The hooked end was just wide enough to fit around a pullet's skinny leg, but too narrow to let the leathery foot escape when the pullet realized it was caught and flushed in panic, screaming the harsh chicken scream, thrashing ineffective wings so the acrid, ammonia-laden dust of the chicken roost rose up to choke its captor.*

*She could feel the panic of those thrashing wings rise in her chest. She fled down the porch steps, carelessly letting the screen door slam behind her. No matter. Mama would find her anyway. She ran for the swing behind the house, knowing her escape, like the pullets', would be futile.*

*She pumped the swing higher and higher, the friendly scrape of rope familiar to her clutched palms, the rush of wind soothing to hot skin. Twin stripes where the ropes tied onto the great limb of the old elm burned white against the bark, like healed scars. The branch shuddered with the motion of the swing, sending a tremble through the canopy of leaves.*

*If she pumped hard enough, maybe she could hear the music before Mama called her. Sometimes, when she reached the apex of the forward swing, the music came to her, like a symphony complete in her head.*

*She had to hurry. Higher and higher, up and back she pumped, trying not to listen for the squawking from the chicken yard, hearing it anyway. Then, her mother's voice.*

*"Chantalene! Come here and help me."*

*No use pretending she couldn't hear. She let the swing die down a few sweeps and bailed out, feeling gravel pebbles on the packed earth through the thin soles of her shoes. She came around the house, dragging her feet, to where Mama stood on the front lawn.*

*Three stunned leghorns hung upside down from each of Mama's hands, the white wings unfurled awkwardly, glassy eyes blinking. Plaintive notes curled up from their open beaks like questions.*

*"Awwk? Errk?"*

*"Here." Mama thrust three pairs of chicken feet into her*

*hands. "Hold them tight. We've got to get six dressed by noon for the Allisons to pick up. Hold these while I kill the others. We've got to hurry."*

*Chantalene grasped the bony feet above the claws, the chickens sagging downward so that their heads dragged the earth. Mama brushed a feather from her damp cheek with the back of her freed arm. She shifted one pullet into her right arm and began to swing it in wide, clock-like circles, her arm extended, careful to keep the chicken from hitting the ground on the downward swing. After half a dozen circles, the bird was stupid with dizziness. It didn't protest when Mama stretched its neck on the ground and planted her foot just behind the head, still holding the feet tightly.*

*She shifted her weight. One quick pull brought the body free from the head, the red, streaming neck cords exposed, brilliant against the white feathers. Mama slung the headless pullet onto the grass, where it flopped wildly, spreading blood on the green lawn. Mama didn't look at it, but began swinging the next chicken.*

*"Don't think about it, just do it," Mama said. "You've got to learn."*

*Obediently, Chantalene swung one of the pullets, over and under like a Ferris wheel. After six swings, her arm aching, she lay the senseless chicken on the ground, placed her foot on its neck. She hesitated.*

*"Pull," Mama commanded. Chantalene pulled, but not hard enough. "Pull hard!" Mama yelled. "Don't make it suffer!"*

*She closed her eyes and pulled with all her might. Suddenly the tension gave way, the body came loose. When she opened her eyes, blood was everywhere. She threw the chicken, letting loose the two in her left hand while the body of the first pirouetted its headless dance across the lawn.*

*She vomited in the grass, and ran.*

*She ran to the swing and pushed off with trembling legs. Higher and higher she pumped, reaching with her legs as the swing pushed upward, leaning forward at the back of the arc. Her narrow hips rose from the wooden seat; her heart flew to her throat. Higher and higher, reaching for the music. She closed her eyes and saw the bloody pullet, flailing, humiliated. She couldn't pump high enough! She couldn't blot out the brutal sight of the dying chicken.*

*Then suddenly she was flying. At the apex of the forward swing, she sailed out of the seat toward the sky—up, toward the music.*

Chantalene jerked upright in bed, gasping. Her heartbeat jolted her chest.

The chicken dream again. *Would the dreams never end?* She forced one deep breath after another until her pulse rate slowed.

Something was dreadfully askew in this dream. Her mother didn't look like herself, didn't act like herself. It was Mama, but it wasn't Mama. LaVita had never raised chickens for sale to the neighbors, only a dozen laying hens that roosted in the shed. And there never had been a chicken house on the place. Yet Chantalene felt that in some incarnation, she had lived that dream.

Stacking her pillows, she collapsed against them but couldn't close her eyes. She focused on familiar shapes in the bedroom to quell the panic—the pale outline of double windows, open to the sounds of the night; the massive silhouette of her black-painted chest of drawers. The room looked much the same as when she was a little girl, before events she couldn't control had twisted her childhood into something bizarre.

She still owned memories from those early years before

her father's trial, and she called on them now like a meditation: shelling peas at the scarred oak dining table with Mama; the fresh green scent when she ran her thumbnail inside the cool pods and popped the tiny globes into a pan. And another: a stream of golden wheat pouring from the spout of a combine, the warm grain covering her bare feet in the bed of the truck.

She had salvaged these moments like gems of broken glass after a disaster. But there were gaps in her memory, as well, that began when she was twelve. Within those voids she had no image of herself or what had happened to her; it was as if she hadn't existed. She was certain her distorted dreams arose from those dark, empty places.

Feeling claustrophobic in the small bedroom, she rose and padded barefoot to the living room, opening the front door to inhale the cool night air.

A low "*Whoof?*" greeted her from outside the screen. Ever vigilant, Bones had heard her movement. The black and white mongrel, picked from a cardboard box of free puppies the semester before she'd abandoned college, swished an invitation with her bushy tail.

"Good idea, girl. I'll come out."

Bones crouched on her hind legs, ears pricked and alert.

"I know what you want, you candy hound. I forgot your treat tonight, didn't I?"

In the kitchen, Chantalene pulled a licorice stick from a crockery jar on the table, then returned to where Bones sat waiting. The screen door squeaked as she stepped onto the cool warped boards of the front porch. Moonlight angled through the railing and patterned the floor with ivory light.

She broke the candy whip in half and shared, sprawling on the porch step with Bones beside her. The dog positioned the licorice upright in her paws, grimacing while she chewed.

Chantalene laughed. “Good stuff, huh?” She scratched the dog’s ears, comforted by the soft fur slipping through her fingers. What would she do without Bones?

A sultry breeze lifted tendrils of her hair and ventilated the over-sized t-shirt she used for a nightgown.

Another night’s rest lost.

Across the moonlit farmyard, Whippoorwill stood sleeping in his corral. The ramshackle wooden fence was more a formality than a barrier for the horse. Part Arabian, Whip had been a high school graduation gift from Monkey Jenks, who’d then boarded him while she went away to school. The Jenkses would have paid for college, too, but Chantalene’s mother had raised her to disdain charity. Monkey and Martha had done enough, taking her in after her mother disappeared, taking her back again and again when she became a teenage runaway. When the county placed her in foster care, Martha and Monkey had even applied to be foster parents, so they could take her back again. She had stayed with them until she finished high school, but no matter how hard they tried Chantalene had never quite been able to accept their parenting. She was painfully aware that she’d repaid their kindness and generosity with nothing but grief.

She would try to atone for that some day. But first she had to untangle her knotted past, despite Martha and Monkey’s well-meaning advice.

She didn’t have to wonder how they would react to her small bit of theater today. They believed the law’s official version—that her father had committed suicide, and her mother abandoned her. Martha had begged her to accept, to forget, to move on.

And for a time she’d tried. She tried to forget everything:

the town, Mama and Daddy, the shards of her childhood that remained. The effort had driven her to the brink of madness. The nightmares had sent her running as a teenager, and they tracked her down in the college dorm, where insomniac nights left her hung-over and enervated, useless for study. A free-floating anger had alienated her from anyone who tried to help.

Even hypnosis hadn't worked. She'd volunteered as a research subject at the University, but whenever the questions got too close to the source of the dreams, she'd awaken. Professor Jackson theorized that her psyche refused to explore some repressed memory. He said she needed counseling, but she'd been there before. Half a dozen social workers had flitted through her teens like ineffectual moths. Even if she did find a therapist who was worth his fee, she couldn't have paid it. Instead she quit school and two part-time jobs to confront her demons alone.

At twenty-four, she felt like Baba Yaga, a thousand years old.

Bones swallowed the last of her licorice and placed her chin on Chantalene's thigh, begging quietly. Chantalene smiled and gave Bones the rest of her candy. Gathering her heavy hair into a ponytail with one hand, she held it up off her damp neck and huffed a sigh.

The sleeping farm looked less forlorn now than on the wind-chilled day last March when she'd stood on the collapsing porch and worried about such basic things as food and shelter. Beyond the corral lay five acres of dried corn stalks and other spent vegetables she'd cultivated the old-fashioned way, without a tractor. She'd sold part of her produce to Bond's Market in Tetumka and the rest on a weekly trip to El Rio, from the back of a truck reluctantly borrowed from Monkey Jenks.

With autumn and winter approaching, the land lay fallow except for her garden beside the house, the hardest work finished until early spring. The labor had thinned and toughened her body and stocked her kitchen shelves with enough home-canning to last the winter.

Beside the corral, a hunched shadow marked the vine-covered remnants of a milking stall—all that remained of a charred shed that had served her parents as a barn. Sitting here one night this summer, she'd recovered a memory of the shed collapsing in flames while she looked back from a fleeing vehicle. Bit by bit, living in the old house had begun to trigger forgotten scenes. She'd learned to steel herself for these brief shocks.

Crickets chorused to one another across the darkness, and her eyes caught the trail of a shooting star in the inky sky. She lay back on her elbows and looked upward, waiting for another. Waiting out the night.

The shrill of the telephone made her jump. Bones scrambled to her feet, looking confused.

*Who could be phoning at this hour?* Mama always said good news never comes in the middle of the night. She hurried to the kitchen phone, goose bumps lacing her arms.

The voice grated like tires on loose gravel. "You want the truth about your daddy, come see me tomorrow."

Chantalene held the receiver away from her ear, repulsed by the sound of an all-too-familiar voice. She set her jaw. "What's in it for you, scum bucket? You know I don't have money."

She heard Willie Bond's subdued laugh, then the unmistakable leer in his final words. "Darlin', I know we can work something out."

"Over my dead body!" But the dial tone buzzed in her ear. "Of course, you probably don't object to necrophilia," she added, and slammed the receiver into its cradle.

But even then she knew—as Willie Bond knew—that she would, indeed, see him tomorrow.

Her hands shook and she folded them under her arms. Would Big Willie Bond be the first to admit her father's hanging wasn't suicide, that the note found in his pocket was planted? A chilling thought. Big Willie headed her list of suspects—the only person she knew of with a reason to want her father dead.

*Why would he call?* Easing a guilty conscience presumed Big Willie had a conscience, and she'd seen no evidence of that. Lecher though he was, even Big Willie wasn't stupid enough to trade incriminating information for sex. And everybody in Tetumka knew she was broke, the forty acres and dilapidated farmhouse she'd inherited encumbered by back taxes. She didn't even own mineral rights to the land.

So what was his motive for luring her to town? Perhaps to silence her questions forever? She'd known from the start that searching for the truth meant gambling safety against sanity.

The old house creaked and she caught her breath, glancing up. The years peeled away and she was ten years old again. Mama stood at the kitchen sink, one bare foot atop the other, smiling as Daddy ambled through the doorway, his chin shadowed with its ever-present dark stubble.

Sometimes the flashbacks nearly stopped her heart. But in a way they were comforting, too—all she had left of her family.

She locked the front door and returned to bed, stripping off her t-shirt. Closing her eyes, she centered her breathing the way she'd taught herself years ago, to combat the terrors. Those nights, trembling and alone, she had discovered a place where shadows of the future fanned out like indecipherable radio waves. Now she thought of it as a pool of psychic energy, but as a girl she'd gone there to sense her mother's presence, like a prayer.

*They were flying down the road in their old sedan. LaVita was taking her to Louisiana to meet Gamma Rose, LaVita's grandmother who'd raised her. It was the summer of Chantalene's tenth birthday, the first and only time she would meet any of her mother's people. Driving east, they were two light-hearted girls, singing out loud with the wind in their hair. Her mother's hair was even longer than hers, and black as oil.*

*Gamma Rose was in her eighties, and she kept the old Gypsy ways. In her house, every person had his own plate, cup, and utensils, with separate ones for guests. An old Gypsy never eats or drinks from any dishes but his own, her mother told her. After supper, they sat around the kitchen table in the tiny, candle-scented house and played cards.*

*Gamma Rose loved cards but disapproved of gambling. Unless, of course, the game was fixed in her favor; then it wasn't gambling at all, but a con, and that was all right. Each face card turned up by her leathery hands cued a story from the past. She had traveled from town to town with the Zingaro Caravan, living by wits and sharp trading. Vignettes flickered inside Chantalene's head like candleflame.*

*In the old days, Gamma Rose said, when a Gypsy woman was about to deliver a baby, the women built a birthing tent apart from the main camp, where the woman bore her child on a handmade straw mattress. Afterward, the tent was burned. LaVita was born in a birthing tent, although the practice was rare by that time. Gypsies didn't value written records, Gamma Rose said, so nobody knew for sure what day she was born or exactly how old she was. When LaVita was old enough to ask, Gamma Rose simply picked out a birthday for her to celebrate.*

*When Gamma Rose told that story, Chantalene watched her mother's eyes recede into the past.*

*In the car on the way home, Chantalene asked, "What happened to your real mother?"*

*"She was married to a man she didn't love and ran away with a man she did, a gadjo," LaVita said, laughing.*

*She told it like a romance, not the tragedy of a mother leaving her child behind. After that, Chantalene kept a secret worry that someday her mother would leave her.*

But LaVita hadn't left her by choice. Chantalene couldn't believe that. She had to know what really happened.

An owl hooted from the elms outside her window, its mournful cry borne on the wind. Chantalene pushed her pillow away, lying flat with her fingers spread on the coolness of the sheet. *Exhale conscious thought; concentrate on your breath ... relax, relax ... .*

Regardless of owls or intuitions, her course was set. Tomorrow morning, after the trickle of early customers at Bond's Market had gone back to their fields and farms, she would ride Whippoorwill into town and make a bargain with the devil.

# THREE

On the official first day of autumn, summer heat bore down on Chantalene's shoulders at mid-morning when she opened the gate to Whippoorwill's corral. Whip accepted his bit and bridle with only a token shake of his head.

She patted his neck. "Good fella." Inhaling his familiar, horsy smell helped calm the growing anxiety in her stomach. His big, petroleum-colored eyes blinked at her while he mouthed the bit into position.

Leading him close to the corral fence, she climbed two railings and mounted up. Her legs perspired inside her black jeans, but she didn't own a saddle and the denim would protect her from the horse's rough hair on the four-mile ride to Bond's Market.

The image of the grocer hunched over the phone in his darkened store last night made her stomach clench. She doubted he'd made the call from home where his wife might overhear. Opal Bond reminded her of a mushroom, living in the dark, devoid of will.

"Let's go, Whip." The horse tossed his head and pranced out of the corral into the farmyard.

Bones began a dance of anticipation. "Sorry, girl," Chantalene told her. "You can't go this time." She gestured toward the house. "Stay, Bones!"

The dog whined, barking once in protest, but reluctantly

took her post on the front porch and watched them clop away.

At the end of the rutted quarter-mile driveway, Chantalene turned Whippoorwill east and put him into an easy trot, wondering again whether she should have brought the shotgun. But that was ridiculous. She couldn't ride into town armed like some Old West outlaw.

Tall grass and sunflowers stood limp along the roadside, needing rain. A welcome breeze lifted her hair.

By the time Whippoorwill's hooves struck the blacktop that marked Tetumka's one-block main drag, their combined shadow bunched shapelessly beneath him. To one side of Bond's Market, a greasy gas pump stood sentinel, and on the other, the glassless windows of two vacant buildings gaped like the mouths of ghosts. One of the buildings had been a beer joint when Chantalene was very young, the other a bank that was closed even then. Not one car or pedestrian animated the street.

Across from the market sat the brick post office, the only other live business in Tetumka. In front, a tattered flag flapped listlessly, its rope clanking against the metal pole. Where the crumbling asphalt street met the sidewalk, the curbs stood full of silt and tickle weeds, shifting in the wind.

Chantalene looped Whippoorwill's reins to the limb of a lone hackberry tree in a weedy vacant lot beside the post office. At this time of day, Thelma Patterson, the postmistress, would have gone home for lunch, or maybe holed up in the back with the air-conditioner blasting.

She crossed the quiet street and pulled open the battered screen door to Willie Bond's domain. Stepping inside, she closed the door quietly behind her and paused to let her eyes adjust to the gloom.

A heavy, offensive smell assaulted her. Spoiled meat? She held her breath, listening.

In the front of the store, wooden shelves held rows of dusty canned goods. Three light bulbs suspended on six-foot cords from a high, stained ceiling were no match for the darkness that collected around the corners of the cavernous room. Above an antique cash register the blades of a 1940s ceiling fan scraped in the silence.

The place was deserted, the locals not yet gathered at the card table in back for their afternoon pitch game. She forced herself to breathe. The wooden floor creaked under her sandals as she passed down the aisle toward the checkout counter.

The cash register stood unguarded. No sign of Big Willie. She moved past it toward the meat counter at the back of the store, an illuminated glass case stocked with stick bologna, chicken parts, and yellow cheese dried up at the edges.

"Mr. Bond?"

No answer. Wind moaned around the wooden windows like a far-away train whistle.

The foul odor rose again and drew her eyes to the meat case. Inside, a listless fly buzzed from a raw chicken neck to a pin-feathered thigh. And on the shadowy floor behind the glass case, she made out the shape of khaki-clad legs, then the waffle-soles of a pair of work boots, toes pointed toward the ceiling.

She inhaled sharply. "Willie?"

On shaky legs she stepped around the meat case and looked down on the sprawled body of Big Willie Bond.

A stained clerk's apron covered the man's bulging stomach and plaid shirt. His beefy arms splayed outward, as if he'd fallen backwards in surprise. But there was no reading the expression on his face, obscured as it was by a coating of fresh blood and a meat saw wedged in his forehead.

A whimper escaped her throat. For a moment her eyes froze on the grisly corpse. A ringing rose in her ears.

She broke and ran toward the front of the store, stumbling, catching herself against the checkout counter by the cash register. The buzzing of the black fly in the meat case filled her head, dimming the lights, and she realized she wasn't breathing.

She forced ragged breaths. When her head cleared, she glanced back toward the meat counter, then at the front door. Her legs wanted to run for it, but her knees voted to dissolve.

"Oh, man," she whined, her voice eerie in the silence. "What do I do now?"

It didn't take long to decide.

No one had seen her. And if anyone did, they'd think she killed him. She had to get out of there.

She hit the screen door at a dead run, knocking it open.

And crashed head-on into a stranger.

"Whoa!" He grabbed her elbows to keep them both from falling. "Sorry. I didn't see you coming ... "

One look at her face stopped his speech. He turned her loose, fast, and backed off. "Are you all right?"

The guy obviously wasn't local; too clean-cut, and he smelled good. But something about him—*the crinkles around dark blue eyes?*—looked distinctly familiar. Where had she seen him before?

Damn. Nothing to do now but tell the truth.

"I'm okay." Her voice shook. "But Willie Bond isn't. He's dead."

"What?"

"In there," she nodded behind her without looking back. "Behind the meat counter. Blood everywhere." Her eyes blinked and she swayed.

He grabbed her arm again. "You'd better sit down." He guided her onto the fender of a silver car, some foreign model, parked at the curb. "Is there a doctor in town?"

"No. Too late anyway."

She'd seen that face before, and heard that voice. Where? She judged him to be early thirties, ten years or so older than she was.

Could this guy have killed Willie Bond? To rob the store, maybe?

But why would he hang around? His face looked tired and innocent. Still, if growing up in Tetumka had taught her anything, it was not to trust appearances.

He seemed to be sizing her up, as well. Then he glanced at the peeling Bond's Market sign on the screen door, turned, and searched the deserted street. His jeans bore a fancy label and the back of his cotton shirt was damp and wrinkled, as if he'd been driving a long time.

He heaved a sigh. "Maybe he isn't really dead," he said, as if speaking to himself. His eyes returned to her, and narrowed. "Wait here. You're not going to pass out, are you?"

Condescending city jerk. "I don't faint," she said flatly.

"Bully for you. I hope I don't."

He glanced up and down the street again, then took a deep breath and disappeared inside the dim interior of the market. The screen door slapped shut behind him.

She sat in the prickling heat, debating. Her stomach churned. Who was this guy? Should she call Sheriff Justin in El Rio?

She ought to call *somebody,* but who would believe her story?

When her knees quit shaking, she stood up. Brushed the dust from the seat of her jeans. Licked her dry lips.

Let old City Slick do it. He seemed like a take-charge

guy. If it weren't for him, she could have made a clean getaway.

She trotted across the street, hoisted herself onto Whippoorwill's back, and lit out for home.

# FOUR

The inside of the country grocery store looked just as Drew Sander remembered it, only smaller, and it smelled worse. Some of those canned goods were dusty enough to have been there since he'd graduated high school and moved away. Back then, though, the place was named Wiedemann's Mercantile.

The floor creaked as he walked toward the meat counter at the back of the store. There he hesitated. He really didn't want to see this, didn't want to deal with it. He had problems of his own.

Gritting his teeth, he stepped around the counter and looked down. *"Jesus H. Christ."*

Revulsion climbed his throat. He pivoted quickly and headed toward the front of the store. At one time, he'd considered studying medicine instead of accounting and law, but had given it up because of a weak stomach. The Little Debbie snack cake he'd eaten on the road about six that morning now threatened a return.

His soon-to-be ex-wife Emily, back in New York, had called him a wimp, among other things, during one of their last fights. Maybe that particular complaint had been accurate. She'd expected him to be some movie version of a cowboy; but of course, he'd harbored some inaccurate expectations, too. If sweet Emily were here, she'd check the dead guy's pockets for cigarettes and sit on his chest to smoke one while she calculated what was in this for her.

Well, maybe that was extreme. She probably wouldn't sit on his chest. Couldn't risk getting blood on a designer skirt.

On the wall near the door, Drew found a white touch-tone telephone, in weird contrast to the nineteenth-century feel of the place. He grabbed the receiver with a sweaty hand and punched the buttons for 911.

Nothing happened. He tried the zero.

"Thank you for using Southwestern Bell," a female voice said, as if he'd had a choice. "May I help you?"

Through a bone-dry mouth, he tried to force a normal voice. "I'm calling from the grocery store in Tetumka. A man appears to have been murdered here."

A pause. "Do you want information?"

"I don't know who I want," he said. "I'm new in town and I don't even know if there's a sheriff here." He did know there was no police station. "Can you help me?"

"I'm not familiar with Tetumka," the voice said, sounding skeptical. "Our office is in Oklahoma City."

"Look, it's close to El Rio," he said, his voice rising. "Can you give me the police in El Rio?"

"One moment, please."

He gripped the receiver and tried to organize his breathing, pushing away the bloody image of the man behind the meat counter. Instead he thought about modern life in these rural hills. An oxymoron.

"The number is 555-3434," the operator said. "You can dial it from there. It's not long distance."

"Thanks a lot," he said, not politely.

Repeating the number aloud, he jabbed the buttons. The phone rang four times before someone picked up. A young male voice promised to notify the sheriff and send a car out. But El Rio was twenty miles away; it would take at least half an hour.

Maybe death waited for no one in the rest of the world, but in Tetumka, even death waited.

The dispatcher took his name. "Please stay there, Mr. Sander, until the sheriff or the medical examiner arrives," he said.

Swell. Drew hung up and pushed through the screen door into the fresh air, praying one more cigarette remained in his last pack, after which he'd sworn to quit. He opened the driver-side door of his car and slumped onto the seat to hunt for it.

Then he remembered the girl.

He got out again and looked around. The tattered flag above the post office fluttered tiredly. Maybe she'd gone in there. Maybe *someone* was in there. He crossed the potholed asphalt.

The front door of the post office was open, giving access to the boxes, but a wooden gate was pulled across the service window. From behind it, a trickle of cool air and the drone of a window unit seeped through from somewhere in the back.

"Anybody here?" He rattled the wooden slats but no one answered. It was only noon, but who around here would complain if they closed early?

Who would *know*?

And who would know if I just split, he thought, instead of waiting around for some official from El Rio?

The girl. But she'd obviously chosen the same option. Could she have been the murderer? Sweat inched down his back.

Naawh. He'd have noticed blood stains on her clothes or hands. Whoever did that to the grocer couldn't have avoided some telltale stains. The girl just followed her natural impulse and fled the scene. He had the same urge. But his respect for the law was ingrained—an unhandy trait in his fast-lane job in the city. Unhandy now, as well, because even while he walked back to the car, weighing his options, he knew damn well he would sit there in the heat and wait.

But he reserved the right to resent it.

He rolled down the windows in the Volvo and opened both doors. It didn't help. His shirt stuck to the seat and the silence made his neck prickle.

So this is what he got for trying to come home again. Thanks a lot, Thomas Wolfe.

With a failed marriage and a stress-wracked job he hated, taking a few weeks off to renovate the family farmhouse for sale had seemed like a great idea. The farmer to whom Drew rented the land had expressed an interest in buying the house, which had sat vacant since his father's death. Drew figured some manual labor in the peace and quiet was just what he needed to unwind, get some perspective, re-chart his future. If he'd wanted murder and mayhem, he could have stayed in New York.

After a long twenty minutes of an unnatural lack of noise, he felt hungry again and desperately thirsty. He scanned the gloomy windows of Bond's Market. No murderer would hang around the scene this long, right?

Inside, he quickly dropped coins in a pop machine and snagged a bag of chips off a metal rack, laying money for the chips beside the register. Behind the counter, rows of cigarette packs beckoned. *What the hell.*

He chose Marlboros, the brand Emily had started him on, and dropped three more dollars on the counter, retreating quickly to the sunshine of the street. In the car again, he leaned back, swung one leg up onto the open door and munched the chips. The salty flavor soothed his stomach.

What a grisly picture. Here he sat feeding his face, on this street where his car looked like an anachronism, and the only other person in town was dead.

Willie Bond, the girl had said.

*How do you do, Mr. Bond? Sorry about your late demise. Or should I say early demise. You weren't all that old and, I'm certain, not ready to die.*

Then he thought about the girl, her face stark white beneath an explosion of blue-black hair. She had smelled like ... what? Licorice? And her eyes held the fight-or-flight look of a wild animal. Deep, dangerous eyes with shadows at the center, like the agate marbles he used to shoot in the schoolyard.

Had she taken off on foot? There were no houses close by except for a few clustered near the Baptist church he'd passed a half-mile outside of town. The rest of the sparse population lived in farm homes scattered miles apart.

For dessert, he lit a cigarette. The first cigarette after he'd quit always tasted fantastic.

His second smoke had burned down to the filter before he finally heard car tires frying on the street. He glanced up, expecting to see a black-and-white, or maybe an ambulance. Instead, he saw a blue Ford pickup with a gun rack in the back window.

*Did killers really return to the scene of the crime?*

The truck parked beside his car and a man wearing Levi's and a faded work shirt stepped out. He stood well over six feet tall, and sweat stains collected around the band of his wide-brimmed hat. Relief filled Drew's stomach when he recognized the man. He got out of his car and hailed him.

"Monkey! Am I glad to see you!"

Montgomery Jenks owned a farm west of Drew's home place and had been his father's closest friend. In fact, Drew's dad had nicknamed him Monkey. "Montgomery" was simply too long to bother with. Drew smiled and stuck out his hand.

Monkey's tanned face opened in a smile. He offered a firm hand, big as a grizzly's paw, but Drew could see Monkey didn't remember him.

"Howdy," Monkey said.

"It's Drew Sander. I've been gone a long time," he added.

"Hell, yes! Matt Sander's boy!" He pumped Drew's hand again and admitted the obvious. "I didn't know you at first."

"I've been sitting here forty-five minutes waiting for the police from El Rio," Drew said, saving the small talk for later. "There's a man in the store who's dead. Murdered, actually."

Monkey bobbed his head and the smile faded. "Yup. The sheriff in El Rio called me." He looked embarrassed. "I guess I'm sort of a deputy around here."

"Oh." Drew paused a moment trying to assess what sort-of-a-deputy meant. But after all, he was in Tetumka. "Well, good." He waited, but Monkey didn't seem to know what to do next, either. "Should we get an ambulance, or the medical examiner, or something?"

"They're sending the doc out from El Rio," Monkey said.

Monkey's speech was so slow Drew found himself holding his breath between phrases, waiting for him to get on with it.

"No telling how long it'll take," Monkey drawled. "They never get in much of a hurry to answer calls out this way."

Drew nodded. "Some things never change."

Monkey gestured toward the store with his head. "Is it Willie Bond?"

"That's what the girl said. I don't know him."

"What girl?"

"Well, not a girl, actually. A young woman. She was running out of the store when I drove up. Guess she discovered the body. I set her on my car and went inside, and when I came out she was gone. Probably got scared and went home."

"Know who she was?"

He shook his head. "Nice looking, early twenties, I'd guess. Black hair, had on a red blouse … ."

Monkey nodded. "Chantalene." He seemed unhappy about something.

"Chantalene?" An unusual name, among the Mary Lous and Donna Kays of southern Oklahoma. But it sounded somehow familiar.

"Got to be," Monkey said. "Only gal with black hair around here since her mama ran off." He paused, then clapped a hand on Drew's shoulder. "Well, let's go take a look at Willie."

Drew couldn't see any need for *him* to look at Willie again, but he didn't argue. He followed Monkey into the musty store.

Monkey's powerful form seemed to part the shadows. "He's back there," Drew offered. "I didn't touch anything."

Monkey leaned over Willie Bond while Drew stayed back and looked away.

"Good Lord Almighty!" Monkey said. Strong language for him. Drew remembered Monkey used to be a deacon in the church, and his wife Martha headed the women's Bible study group. Another condition he bet hadn't changed.

Monkey straightened, wiping his hands on a red bandanna though he hadn't touched the corpse. "It's *Big* Willie. I was expecting Little Willie." His weathered face pleated around a frown.

"Little Willie?"

"His son's grown, but everybody calls him Little Willie." He stuffed the bandanna back in his hip pocket. "Well, he didn't do that to hisself," Monkey observed. "Poor old Willie. Had a hard life and a hard death. Obnoxious cuss, but nobody deserves this."

A country man's benediction.

At the front of the store, Monkey helped himself to a cold pop and offered to buy one for Drew. Drew declined, the last one still sloshing in his stomach. They went outside and stood in the narrow shade of the building while Monkey drank his orange soda.

"I don't remember any Bonds living around Tetumka," Drew said.

"They moved here," Monkey paused to calculate, "maybe fifteen years back. Not long after you left, I guess. Willie and his wife had five kids, and not much luck controlling any of 'em. Little Willie's the only one that still lives at home, though." He shook his head. "Mrs. Bond'll take this hard. She's a whiner anyway." It didn't sound like criticism coming from Monkey, just a statement of fact.

The car from El Rio finally arrived, a beat-up ambulance with two men inside. The driver was a gangly kid who didn't look old enough to have a license, let alone wear the deputy sheriff's uniform of Opalata County. But then, ever since Drew passed thirty, kids had started looking younger. The other man, in his early sixties, Drew guessed, was bald as a peeled onion and almost as white. Obviously he didn't spend much time hatless in this sun. He carried a black bag in his hand.

"Hi, Doc," Monkey said.

"Mr. Jenks," the doctor said, nodding. The kid seemed used to being ignored. His dark hair was cut in a homemade burr and there was a fresh crease in the khaki pants, as if they'd never been worn before. A shadow on his upper lip foretold the inadequate beginnings of a moustache.

The doctor's lined face carried a practiced, matter-of-fact expression, but the small gray eyes were sharp and intelligent. "Have a patient for me?"

"Have a dead one," Monkey responded. "He's inside."

Neither the doctor nor the deputy glanced at Drew. Now these were city folk—no eye contact. He felt right at home.

It didn't seem an appropriate time for Drew to leave yet—as if he were fleeing the murder scene—so he filed inside behind the others. They paused a moment to let their eyes adjust to the dusky interior, then Monkey led the medical examiner to Willie Bond's corpse while Drew watched from a distance.

The doctor put on thin plastic gloves and crouched to examine the body. "Get the camera," he said to the young deputy, without looking up.

The kid, with the medical examiner coaching him, took pictures of the corpulent carcass first from his right side, then his left, then a close-up of the head wound.

There's no privacy in death, Drew thought.

He averted his eyes while the doc removed the meat cutter, carefully wrapping it in plastic supplied by his assistant, who now appeared quite interested in his work.

The doc switched on a portable tape recorder in his front shirt pocket and began a monologue as he took off one of Willie Bond's boots and his sock and checked the toes. To estimate the time of death, Drew supposed, but he couldn't decipher the doctor's flat monotone without leaning closer. Instead, he walked to the back and used the restroom, which proved almost as repulsive as the scene behind the meat counter.

While the doc finished and Monkey took notes in a tiny

book with the stub of a pencil, Drew wandered outside and leaned against the building in a small strip of shade. Wherever that black-haired girl had gone, he wished he'd gone with her.

Finally Monkey and the kid rolled a stretcher outside and slid Willie Bond's bagged bulk inside the ambulance. Drew felt relieved when they closed the doors.

The doctor joined them and put his black bag behind the front seat of the car. The three of them stood beside the ambulance in the heat, casual as if they were discussing next year's crop, and watched the deputy rope off Bond's Market with yellow crime-scene tape.

"I'll send the autopsy report to Sheriff Justin," the doc said. "He said to tell you he'd be out as soon as he could and go over the scene. He was in court today and couldn't get loose."

Monkey nodded. "What do you think, Doc?"

Doc's eyes betrayed a slight twinkle. "I think somebody didn't like him much. No witnesses, I guess?" For the first time, he looked directly at Drew.

"He was a goner when I got here." Drew's lapse into country dialect sounded ridiculous even to him. He felt his face redden and was about to add that the girl might have seen something, but Monkey cut in.

"I'll drive out to tell his family." Monkey folded his arms and squinted toward the empty street. "Mrs. Bond'll want to know if she can see him."

The doc grimaced, wrinkling his bald forehead halfway up his scalp, which already was turning pink in the sun. "Not right away, since you've already ID'd him. She'll have to call the funeral parlor to come pick him up after the autopsy, though. Undertaker will need to do some work on him before he's fit for the family to see."

The deputy set a beat-up wooden chair from the market in the narrow strip of shade on the sidewalk in front and retrieved a rifle from behind the seat of the ambulance. He took up his post, the weapon horizontal on his crossed legs, apparently guarding the scene of death until a real sheriff came along to investigate.

Monkey and the doctor shook hands. "Thanks for coming out," Monkey said.

Doc climbed behind the wheel and the ambulance lurched over prairie-dog-sized potholes as it drove away. Drew hoped Big Willie had his seat belt on.

Monkey leaned against the tailgate of his pickup and pulled out his tobacco.

"Chew?" He tilted the pouch toward Drew.

"No, thanks." Drew pulled out a cigarette and lit it. "What I could really use, after that, is a stiff drink."

Monkey allowed a crooked smile. "Can't get one around here."

"Why not? Didn't Oklahoma finally pass liquor-by-the-drink?"

"Yup, county option." He poked a wad of brown leaves inside his jaw. "But this is a dry county. Ladies' church group even gave Willie fits for stocking three-two beer in the market. But Willie was more afraid of their husbands, if he *quit* selling it."

Monkey's wheezy chuckle sounded like the Deputy Dog cartoon character Drew used to watch as a kid. He'd forgotten that infectious laugh. He laughed, too, for the first time that day. Hell, the first time in weeks.

"This place may be more fun than I can stand," Drew said. "No bars, no booze, just falling bodies."

"Yup. We're dead serious," Monkey allowed, wheezed another laugh and folded the tobacco pouch back into his pocket. He squinted after the ambulance where it had rounded a curve and disappeared in a cloud of dust. "Want to ride out to see Chantalene with me?"

Drew was surprised. He'd have expected Monkey to see the Bonds first, but then he remembered this was a reluctant deputy. And Monkey always did do things his own way.

"If you want me to," Drew said. He *was* curious about that wild-looking young woman.

"Suit yourself," Monkey said.

They rode with the windows down, the hot wind and deep rumble of the engine bringing Drew memories of teenage summer nights with his buddies, in search of excitement they seldom found. Usually they wound up tracking their fathers' pickup tires over hapless tarantulas that ventured onto the shale roads leading home from El Rio.

Monkey drove in silence, turning left one mile past the turn-off to Drew's family's farm.

"What's her last name?" Drew asked.

"Morrell."

"Clyde Morrell's girl? They used to live on the back of the same section our place is in, straight through behind Animal Draw."

Monkey spat tobacco out his open window. "That's the one."

"I'd forgotten they had a daughter. We never saw much of them."

"That's Chantalene," Monkey said. "Her daddy killed hisself twelve years ago; mama took off after that. County tried to put the girl in foster homes, but she kept runnin' off. Finally they let her stay with us, and Martha looked after her as much as Chantalene would let her."

"Didn't she have any relatives?"

"None she'd admit. She was with us on and off for several years, and moved away a stranger. Lives out here by herself now."

"Poor kid," Drew said. "No wonder she got scared and ran away today."

Monkey humphed. "Chantalene may be a lot of things, but scared ain't one of 'em."

Drew looked at him, but Monkey didn't elaborate.

They turned left again onto a long, rutted dirt driveway that led to the Morrell place. The truck bounced like a mechanical bull.

Drew recalled the Morrells as a strange couple, never well accepted by the community. They kept to themselves except when Clyde went on a drinking binge. Then he'd rage into town, bellowing things nobody understood and tearing up anything in his way. But this didn't happen often, so generally folks left them alone. People said Mrs. Morrell—an attractive dark-haired woman whose name Drew couldn't recall—was a Gypsy, and that Clyde had made a trip east and brought her home as his bride. Others doubted they were really married. She was much younger than Clyde, and Drew remembered his own mother and grandmother speculating on why any woman would marry Clyde Morrell. They had no children for years, and then came the baby girl. Clyde wouldn't take his wife to a hospital and she'd given birth at home, while Clyde went into town and got drunk.

Or so the gossip went.

Twice Drew had ridden over here with his dad to tell Clyde his hogs were out, and the farm had looked like a junkyard.

But today the Morrell property was tidy, with a patch of grass in front of the house neatly trimmed. Red and white petunias flourished in two window boxes on the front porch, in open defiance of obvious hard times. The small frame house appeared to lean with the south wind. Its roof was patched with pieces of tin nailed down at the edges, and all but a hint of white paint had long ago flaked away.

In a corral across the driveway from the house, a thin gray horse watched them drive up, its ears flicking forward in lazy interest. Drew recognized it as the one he'd seen in the vacant lot next to the post office. So that was how Chantalene had gotten home.

There was no garage on the place and, as far as he could see, no car. The field beyond was tangled with various wilted row crops.

Furious barking greeted them from the front porch of the house. Monkey climbed out and spoke to a black and white dog in a gentle voice.

"Hey, Bones. Take it easy, girl."

Hackles raised, the dog answered with a growl, but at the sound of a voice from inside the house, it ceased barking and wagged its tail. Only then did Drew get out of the pickup.

Chantalene Morrell stepped outside. She wore the same red peasant blouse he'd seen that morning, now with black shorts. Her legs were slender and tanned, and her hair glistened like jet in the sunlight.

"Hello, Chantalene," Monkey said. He took the battered hat into his hands.

"Hello, Monkey. I figured you'd come." She aimed a glance at Drew as if he'd betrayed her.

"You could come in," she said to Monkey. "Have some iced tea." Drew wasn't sure the invitation included him.

"Thank you kindly. Maybe another day," Monkey said. "Just want to ask you a couple questions."

The girl sank onto the top step of the porch, hugging her knees.

Monkey looked down at his boots and then out toward the horse. "Whippoorwill needs some oats," he remarked.

"He'll have to get by on grass."

Monkey paused a beat. She wasn't going to help him out. "Were you in the store this morning?"

"You know I was." Again the accusing glance at Drew.

"Want to tell me about it?"

"I don't have much choice, do I?" She drew a breath and exhaled it in a sigh. "I needed a few groceries. He was dead when I got there, around eleven-thirty."

The dog snuggled close to her and Drew noticed the way she massaged its ears, not for her enjoyment, but for the dog's. He got the definite impression she liked animals more than people.

"Big Willie still bothering you?" Monkey asked, not meeting her eyes.

"Not anymore, I guess." She shrugged. "But I didn't kill him. Of course, nobody will believe that." She brushed a strand of hair from her eyes.

"You see anybody else around? Anybody see you?"

"Just him," she said, tipping her head toward Drew.

Monkey nodded. "This is Drew Sander. Owns the Sander place, straight behind yours."

"Hello," Drew said.

"I know who he is," she said without shifting her glance from Monkey.

*How could she know?*

"Well," Monkey paused. "Guess I'd better call on Mrs. Bond." His voice sounded heavy.

"Tell Martha thanks for the homemade bread," she said.

Monkey nodded. "She remembered how much you used to like it. Maybe you ought to call her, tell her yourself."

"I know," she said, but her tone said she wouldn't do it. And despite the tension of Monkey's questioning, a look of understanding passed between them.

They were almost back to the pickup when she called out.

"Monkey? Do you have to tell anybody? That I was there?"

"Afraid so, Chantalene," he said. "Been my experience, the truth's always the best way to go."

Her smile was humorless. "Since when has this town cared for truth?"

Monkey didn't answer that one.

Looking back as the truck bucked away, Drew thought he'd never seen a face so resigned to trouble. For his first eighteen years, the Morrells had been his closest neighbors, yet he knew nothing about this girl and hadn't known of her father's death. The thought brought on an odd niggling of guilt. Emily would have said he was too centered on screwing up his own ordinary life to take notice of anyone else's.

He was damn sick of Emily's voice yammering inside his head. Especially when it was right.

# FIVE

From her front porch, Chantalene watched Monkey Jenks' pickup truck lumber down her driveway, turn onto the shale road, and pick up speed. A funnel of red dust boiled up behind the truck, and her stomach echoed its rolling motion.

*He'll be back. Probably with the sheriff. Damn!*

And damn Drew Sander, too. If it hadn't been for him, she could have escaped from Bond's Market without anyone knowing she'd been there.

What was Sander doing back here, after all these years? She'd been too frazzled to recognize him after finding Willie Bond's body, but riding home she'd managed to place the face. He looked a lot like she remembered his father, Matt. She hadn't seen or heard of Drew Sander since he'd gone away to college, when she was still in grade school. Now, thanks to his untimely reappearance, she'd be a prime suspect for murder.

And that wasn't even the scariest part. Who *did* kill Big Willie, and why?

The image of Willie Bond's corpse returned to her in deadly color. She shivered. She would bet the farm someone killed him because he'd threatened to tell her the truth. If she was right, then she was at least partly responsible for his death.

Much as she despised Big Willie, she hadn't set out to

incite a killing. Still, she should have expected a violent reaction when she threatened to expose the guilty. If whoever hanged her father was willing to kill again to protect the secret, why hadn't he—or more likely *they*—targeted her instead of Willie Bond? Perhaps Big Willie's murder was intended to serve two purposes—eliminate the loose cannon, and scare her away. If she didn't back off, it stood to reason they'd come after her next.

And she still didn't know who t*hey* were.

A peculiar and chilling feeling, to think that someone wanted her dead. She pushed it out of her mind, casting about for some physical chore to calm her nerves. She had to think. Had to make a plan.

She retrieved a load of clean laundry from her old washer and carried the basket to the clothesline in the backyard. Anchoring red shirts on the line beside her black jeans and shorts, her hands became her mother's hands—her black hair her mother's, blowing in the wind. Her earliest memory—she couldn't have been more than three—was of sitting in the wicker clothesbasket, watching LaVita pin clothes onto the windy sky.

A sharp ache stitched her chest, hollowing her out with a sense of loss. She missed her mother's laugh and freewheeling spirit most of all. LaVita could have taught her about her Gypsy heritage, about being a woman, about *having fun.* Standing among the wind-whipped clothes on the line, Chantalene felt cheated, and the familiar anger rose hot in her throat.

She had to know what really became of LaVita, and who killed her father. Someone had destroyed her family—why? Regardless of Willie Bond's death, regardless of anything else that might happen, she had to know the truth. If the guilty ones were killing each other, why should she care?

But perhaps she couldn't do it alone—not and stay alive.

She knew beyond doubt that she'd be seeing Sheriff Justin soon. He would want to question her about Big Willie. What if she called the sheriff before he called her, and asked for his help? Would he believe her?

Not likely. He was ethical enough to send her the letter from McAlester prison, but Sheriff Justin remembered her as the runaway, the delinquent teenager. They had some unfortunate history together, and she knew he'd view anything she told him with skepticism. He wouldn't re-investigate a twelve-year-old crime based on suspicions; he'd demand facts. Especially since re-opening the case meant he'd been wrong not to investigate Clyde's death as a homicide at the time.

Someone knew the truth. She had to find out who—and get him to talk.

She glanced toward the West, gauging the sun. An hour before sundown. All the old farmers were always home by dark. Including Slim Jenks.

She changed into jeans again and bridled Whippoorwill for the second time that day. Mounting up, she called out to Bones. "Stay, Bones. Guard the house." She kept her voice friendly so as not to alarm the dog, but dread had settled like Texas chili in her stomach.

Bones whined, crushed at being left behind again, but she obeyed.

Slim Jenks' ranch lay six miles east toward the hazy Black Fork Mountains. Though Chantalene had never been to his place before, everybody knew where Slim lived. She urged Whippoorwill into an easy trot and relaxed the reins while the evening cooled and the sun slid toward the horizon. Her rear bounced against the horse's bare back.

She pictured Slim Jenks at the Selby farm, his face turning white when he met her eyes, the willow dowsing rod slipping from his hands. Slim was superstitious, no doubt; she knew his brother Monkey was. But even if Slim believed Opal Bond's gossip about Chantalene inheriting "witchy powers" from her mother, she doubted that would cause him to deflate the way he did yesterday. The only other explanation she could fathom for his odd reaction was guilt.

Slim had the reputation of a gentle giant. She recalled a story about his rescuing a den of coyote pups another farmer had found and intended to kill. Slim took the pups home and raised them as pets until they grew up and wandered back into the wild. What if a man with such a kind heart knew about her father's murder, knew who the lynchmen were? Years of covering up such a secret might eat a man of conscience alive. And might cause him grief at the sight of the murdered man's daughter.

It was the only lead she had. Perhaps Slim knew the truth and was ready to tell it.

Dust powdered up from beneath Whippoorwill's hooves. By the time they passed the rural mailbox marked S. Jenks, Chantalene's tailbone was sore and her stomach tense. She turned Whip into Slim's driveway and slowed the horse to a walk.

Dusk collected in the thick canopy of trees shrouding the small farmhouse of Tetumka's fiddle-playing, water witching, lone bachelor. On the narrow front porch, a scrawny yellow tomcat peered at her with luminous eyes, mewling in open-mouthed alarm. Two more strays peeked from beneath the step, and her skin prickled with the certain weight of dozens of other eyes watching from hidden places.

Whippoorwill's hooves thudded on hard-packed dirt as they neared the house. She reined to a halt in the dooryard and called out.

"Halloo!"

She sat the horse a moment, waiting. "Halloo! Anybody home?"

She dismounted and dropped the reins to the ground. The horse stood. Somewhere within the house a light came on, illuminating curtained windows with a dull glow. Chantalene waited without approaching the porch. Long moments passed before the front door creaked open behind the screen and she made out Slim's lanky shadow outlined in lamplight. A mourning dove crooned in the silence.

"It's Chantalene Morrell."

"I see it is," his deep voice returned.

"I'd like to talk to you."

He stood for a long time with one hand poised on the open door. She began to think he would close it and disappear into the house again.

"Just talk, that's all," she said inanely. "I think you could answer some questions for me."

Another pause. "I can't ask you in," he said finally, his bass rumble so deep she could barely distinguish the words. "Wouldn't be fittin'."

She nodded. A country bachelor of his generation wouldn't think it appropriate to invite a single woman into his house.

"Will you come out?" she said.

The screen door scraped open and Slim ducked under the doorway as he stepped outside. The door thumped shut behind him. Poised on the tiny porch in the dusk, his thin body curved like a question mark. He motioned in silence toward two metal lawn chairs in the yard, spaced a respectful distance apart beneath the overhanging branches of an oak. She followed him into the shadows.

Leaves, felled prematurely by summer's intense heat, littered the chair seats. Slim brushed them aside and waited until she sat before he lowered himself into the other chair. Despite his height, the spring-style chair barely squeaked beneath him. Even his graying hair was thin.

He did not look at her. A full moon had risen above the sleeping, tree-covered hills, and in the splotches of moonlight sifting through the leaves she caught glimpses of his pale face. He was only a few years older than Monkey, maybe sixty-one or two, but tonight he looked older than sin.

The evening air cooled her damp shirt, sending a shiver over her skin.

Slim's voice rumbled beneath the darkness. "I figured you'd come. Eventually."

A cicada tuned up on a branch above their heads and lightning bugs arose from the grass like tiny lanterns.

"Then you know what I want to ask," she said, and waited.

"I'm real sorry about your daddy. Everybody thought he had ... " Slim paused, unable to say the word *rape,* "ruined that poor little girl, and her too simple-minded to tell."

Chantalene stiffened in her chair. *"But he didn't."* She held her breath, the cicada's thrum pulsing inside her head.

"All the evidence pointed to Clyde. When he was acquitted, we thought he'd got away with it." His voice trembled. "If you'd seen that little girl ... all bruised up ... defenseless."

Silhouetted against the deepening blue sky, a bullbat cried out in its nightly hunt. Chantalene fought the anger that hammered against her chest and kept her voice low. "Who hanged my father?"

She heard him inhale, a rattling breath.

"I won't tell you that." His voice gathered strength. "Vengeance belongs to the Lord."

"It wasn't the Lord who killed Big Willie Bond."

He was silent for a while. "The Lord works in mysterious ways. Beware what you meddle with, Miss Morrell."

"You don't think I have a right to know who killed my father?"

His voice filled with sorrow. "What good would it do? You'd just hurt yourself with the knowledge. And you've been hurt enough." Shadows hid his face. Only the toes of his worn cowboy boots protruded into moonlight. "The guilty always pay for their sins. Sooner or later."

*Bullshit,* Chantalene thought, but didn't say it. "At least tell me what happened to my mother. *Please.*"

He shook his head slowly. "I don't know. She must've feared for her life and kept on runnin'."

Her stomach clenched at the familiar refrain. "She would have come back for me! My mother was not a coward."

"No, she wasn't," he said slowly. "And she took her own revenge."

Chantalene leaned forward, the metal chair rocking beneath the shift in weight. "What do you mean?"

Slim didn't answer. Instead, she heard a choked sound in his breathing, felt him tense in the chair.

"Mr. Jenks? Are you all right?" She peered at him in the darkness, started to rise.

"Yesterday, when I saw you, I thought she'd come back." He coughed, a wrenching, painful sound. "I haven't been well. You'll have to excuse me."

Slim Jenks unfolded from the chair and without another word made his way unsteadily back into the house.

She sat alone in the shifting shadows beneath the tree, her eyes burning, the ache in her chest almost unbearable.

*Heavy footsteps on the hollow wooden floor of the old farmhouse; one quick shout from her father, then silence. She sat up in her bed, straining to hear the mumbled voices.*

*Instead, a thump—like a body—shook the living room wall. Her mother's groan, not loud, subdued. Chantalene threw her legs over the side of the bed, and stood up, her heart pounding.*

*Socko growled. A deep voice, unrecognizable, returned the threat. Then footsteps scraped out the front door, down the porch steps. It was all over in seconds. Nothing left but Socko's frenzied barking in the silence.*

When the yellow rectangle of light from Slim's window went dark, she rose heavily from the chair, mounted Whippoorwill, and headed home.

Moonlight washed the road ahead in ivory light. Her breath came hard around the tightness in her chest.

Slim Jenks had helped murder her father. It had been written all over the old man's face. She was certain of the knowledge, but instead of setting her free, the truth made her sick at heart.

And still, she had no proof.

She let Whip walk home at his own pace. It was close to midnight when they turned off the road onto her driveway, and too late to run by the time she saw the white car hunched in the shadow of a mulberry tree beside the corral.

Someone was waiting for her.

# SIX

Chantalene halted Whippoorwill and stared at the white car. In the moonlight, she caught the glitter of a gold shield on its door—the Opalata County Sheriff's Department shield.

Sheriff Justin hadn't wasted any time. *Damn.*

Still, facing the sheriff wasn't nearly as scary as what she'd first feared—a visit from Willie Bond's murderer.

She thought of turning her horse and fleeing. But that was futile. Justin undoubtedly had watched her approach for a quarter mile, and Whip couldn't outrun his car. Sighing, she tapped her heels to the horse's sides and they plodded ahead.

The vehicle must have been there quite a while, because Bones had stopped barking and taken up a position a dozen feet from the driver's side door. Lying on her stomach, panting but watchful, Bones turned her head toward the sound of Whippoorwill's hooves.

Whip walked into his pen without urging, grateful to be home. Chantalene slid off his back and removed the bridle. She heard the car door open and the wheeze of springs as Sheriff Justin extracted himself from behind the wheel. Bones got up and began to bark.

She tended to the horse and hung the bridle on a nail inside the lean-to beside the corral, taking her time. When she turned toward the house, Sheriff Justin was leaning against the corral gate. She hadn't seen him for more than two years. He looked a bit heavier, but otherwise unchanged.

"Don't you feed that skinny nag?" he said quietly. "It'd have to stand beside itself twice to cast a shadow."

His voice in the stillness sent Bones into a frenzy of noise. Chantalene called out to quiet her, and Bones grudgingly resorted to sporadic woofs.

"He's not a nag. He's a gelding," she said. "Can't you tell the difference?"

"He's still skinny," the sheriff said. Whippoorwill snuffled, moved to the horse tank, and lowered his head to drink.

"How've you been, Chantalene? You're looking good."

From the sheriff, the words held no innuendo; she'd never known him to have anything but business on his mind. A circle of shadow from his wide-brimmed hat hid his eyes, but below that, the leathery face looked familiar. Moonlight cast shadows across the sharp creases of his khaki pants.

"Thanks. You've put on some weight," she observed.

He shifted to keep an eye on Bones, who circled him warily. "I hope your watchdog don't decide to ventilate the back end of my brand new uniform."

"Quiet, Bones," she said again, without conviction. Could she help it if Bones plain didn't like the man?

The top rail of the corral fence swayed as Chantalene leaned against it. "Is this a social call, then, in the middle of the night?"

Bones laid her ears back and growled.

Sheriff Justin took off his hat and slid the rim through in his hands. "Not exactly. I need you to answer some questions."

"Do I need a lawyer?"

"Did you kill him?"

"You want me to just *tell* you and take all the fun out of your investigation?"

She heard herself reverting to the role of rebellious teenager she'd always played in his presence, but she couldn't stop. Back then she'd learned to cover fear with bravado. And at this moment, with her nerves flayed by the eerie encounter with Slim Jenks, her stomach rolled like an avalanche. Luckily, with no lunch and no supper, it held nothing to eject.

The sheriff shook his head, studied the hat brim in his hands. "With you, it's always got to be the hard way, doesn't it?"

She didn't answer. She took a deep breath, then another, trying to stop the flow of adrenaline that always made her crazy.

The sheriff sighed, stood up straight and replaced the hat. "All right then. I'm taking you in to El Rio for questioning in the death of William Bond. Get in the car."

Her adrenaline surged. *"Tonight?"*

The alarm in her voice brought Bones to her feet again, snarling.

The sheriff stood his ground, his face hard. "Tonight." His hand went to his holster. "And call off that nasty-tempered mutt or it'll be buzzard food."

The night was sultry and the windows in Sheriff Justin's squad car wouldn't roll down. The air conditioning didn't quite reach the back seat, which smelled faintly of antiseptic and vomit. Chantalene cringed at the thought of what other outlaw legs had stuck to the plastic seat covers before hers. By the time they reached El Rio, she was dead tired, hungry, and her t-shirt stuck to her back. She'd developed an attitude.

Sheriff Justin put his hand under her elbow like a prom date and escorted her through the deserted reception area to his stark cubicle of an office. It was even stuffier than the car. His wall clock showed twenty minutes past midnight. She slouched into the wooden chair across from his desk and pulled her hair up off her neck, fuming.

A young deputy, who seemed to be the only other person on duty at this hour, followed them into the office and handed the sheriff a file folder, winking. "Want me to handcuff her to the chair?"

"In your fantasies," Chantalene snapped.

"That won't be necessary, Bobby," the sheriff said dryly. "But it wouldn't hurt to keep an eye on the front door, in case she bolts."

When they were alone, she reached for a rubber band from the top of his desk. He caught her wrist.

"It's for my hair!" she said. "I swear I won't kill myself or anybody else with it."

He let go, frowning.

While he studied the contents of the file, she wound the band four times around a ragged ponytail at the back of her neck, then sat back in the chair and puffed a sigh. "You can't seriously think I murdered Willie Bond."

"What I think doesn't have much to do with it at this point. You were at the scene. Your motives are common knowledge. And the Bonds are frothing at the mouth for us to file charges."

"So you caved in to pressure from the likes of Little Willie and Opal Bond?"

"Don't mess with me, Chantalene. If you hadn't pulled that stunt at the water-witchin' none of this would have happened."

So. The Tetumka grapevine was in working order.

"At the very least," he said, "you're a material witness.

I have to question you, and you could have made things easier by coming in voluntarily."

She shrugged. "So question. But I'm *not* a witness. I told Monkey everything I know the other day ... ." Her voice trailed away. Sheriff Justin's presence always had affected her like a polygraph.

"What else?" He leveled gray eyes at her, and she swallowed back a smart-ass response and reminded herself she was an adult now, and this was no runaway incident; this was murder.

With several years' perspective, she could admit the sheriff had treated her as kindly back then as she and the law would allow. But the fact remained that he had certified her father's death as suicide—and Sheriff Justin didn't like to be wrong. He also didn't like folks stirring up trouble in his quiet little circle of influence. Her heat-induced bluster softened.

"Big Willie phoned me the night before he was killed," she said.

"What time?"

"Around midnight, I'd guess. Maybe later. I don't exactly live by clocks these days."

Sheriff Justin waited.

"He said if I wanted the truth about my father, to come see him."

"And you said you would?"

"No. But he knew I would."

The sheriff nodded. "Do you know where he called from? Anybody with him?"

She shook her head. "I didn't hear anybody."

"Anybody else call you?"

"No. I went to bed and the next morning I rode Whippoorwill to town."

"Tell me exactly what you saw, and what you did, every

detail," he said. "You never know what might turn out to be important."

So she told him, deliberately including every sight and sound and smell to prove she was trying to cooperate.

"You didn't see anybody in the store or on the street, either before or after you found Willie?"

"Just Sander, like I said, when I ran out."

"What about Thelma Patterson?"

"I didn't see her. I assumed she was in the back of the post office, but there's a carport behind it where she always parks. I couldn't see it from where I left Whip, so I don't know for sure she was there. Have you talked to Thelma? Maybe she saw someone in town before I got there."

The sheriff gave her a dark look: *Don't tell me my job.* "Thelma says she can't see the street from inside her office, and with her air conditioner running she can't even hear cars come and go."

Chantalene smiled. "I'll bet she hates that."

Justin gave her another look. "The rural carrier left to make his route about nine and no customers came in all morning. Thelma went home for lunch at eleven-thirty, but she left the back way and didn't see anybody."

"Swell. So what's next?"

He appeared to think it over.

"Look," she said. "I'll take a lie detector test. I didn't kill Willie Bond."

He handed her a yellow tablet and a ballpoint pen. "Write out a complete statement, just like you told it to me, starting with Willie Bond's phone call. Make sure you don't leave anything out. Then sign your name." He cleared a place for her to work on the edge of the desk. "I'll be right back."

When he'd gone, Chantalene allowed herself a short string of curse words, then wiped her damp palms on her jeans and began to write. In a few minutes Sheriff Justin came back in and sat in his squeaky desk chair while she finished. She signed her name and handed him the tablet and pen.

"Will somebody drive me home now?"

He looked at the tablet instead of her. "Not just yet. We're going to give you a temporary room at our lovely little hotel here." A muscle in his jaw twitched, and he held up a hand to stall her objections. "Look, Chantalene, you've got motive, opportunity, and no alibi. And your history doesn't give me much confidence you wouldn't skip town if I let you go."

"I can't believe you'd—"

"Also," he added, stopping her again, "there's the matter of your own safety. I can't have you out there in that house alone, with Little Willie and an unknown killer on the loose."

Anger sharpened her tone. "You're not responsible for my safety."

"If I'm not, who will be? You don't appear to give it much thought yourself." He fingered the corners of a file folder as the young deputy came in the room again. "Bobby's gonna take you upstairs."

She felt a shiver cross her neck, but her face flushed hot. *Shit,* she thought. *Shit, shit, shit.*

# SEVEN

The deputy guided her out of Sheriff Justin's office and down the hallway to the elevators. It wouldn't be the first night Chantalene had ever spent in jail, but she was a teenager then and they'd put her in the juvenile facility across the street. Juvie hall wasn't pretty, but it was a Marriott compared to the Opalata County Jail.

On the third floor, a woman in uniform met them at the elevator. "This way," she said.

Chantalene appealed to the deputy with her eyes. "Oh, man! You've got to be kidding."

"Sorry," the deputy said, and even managed to look as though he meant it. "Regulations."

The woman, stone-faced and fortyish, didn't speak until they were alone in a small room with no windows.

"Everything off," she said.

When your life sinks to a certain level, Chantalene reflected, you become grateful for the smallest things. Standing naked in the austere room, she appreciated the matron's bored demeanor. If the woman had seemed interested, she'd have had to deck her, and the matron was built like a wrestler.

At least they let her keep her own clothes. When she was dressed again, the matron led her to a locked, barred door. Beyond stretched a row of cells right out of a 1950s movie.

The county lock-up consisted of a dozen cells for men and two for women, separated from each other by the jailer's desk and two sets of iron doors. Chantalene glanced down the men's wing and saw two tenants, one an elderly man who snored as if he were sleeping off a drunk. The other was hard-looking and young, his hairless arms covered from shoulder to knuckle with multi-colored tattoos. His head was shaved except for a strip down the middle that ended in a dirty ponytail in back. The kid's listless gaze met hers but didn't linger. Lucky for him. She felt mean enough to bite through the bars and claw out his eyes.

They passed one empty cell and the matron opened the barred door of the second. There was a cot with a rough-looking brown blanket, a rust-stained lavatory, and a half-wall beside the john that concealed it from fellow inmates. From the front, however, the seat afforded an open view of the hallway. The matron said nothing as she clanged the door shut, locked it, and left Chantalene alone.

The cinder block walls felt cool as a cave. Goose bumps stood up on her bare arms, and her rough breathing echoed against the walls in the reeking silence.

For the first hour, she sat rigid on the sagging cot and relived the terror of an alienated teenager on her first night of lock-up. That night, frightened and dirty, she'd stayed awake until daylight, weeping.

*They can't make me cry this time.*

She wrapped herself in the coarse blanket and lay down, exhausted. For a long time she listened to the distant sleeping noises of the old man and the space cadet, her fellow prisoners. Only in the intense darkness closest to sunrise did she finally doze. And then the dreams came.

*Four hooded figures loomed before her, their feet hidden in a cloud-like mist. She crouched lower in tall grass, watching, her heart hammering against her chest.*

*Three of the specters walked together, one slightly behind—different from the rest, in charge.*

*When she could stand it no longer, she cried out from her hiding place. "Where is my mother? Where is my daddy?"*

*Again and again, she called. The shadows didn't answer, didn't seem to hear.*

*"Don't ever tell anyone what you saw!" Her mother's voice.*

*She stood up. "Mama! Daddy! Don't leave me!"*

*The four shrouded figures turned toward her as one. Their hoods gaped open, revealing dark, featureless ovals where the faces should have been. They advanced toward her, menacing, obscene.*

*"Run, Chantalene! Run!" Again her mother's voice. "Don't ever tell anyone!"*

Her eyes jerked open, her scream echoing against the stone walls. For a moment she was disoriented, then recognized the high window where pale light angled down through glass and bars. Her stomach cramped and she was shaking.

She pulled the blanket tighter around her and coached her breathing back to normal.

This time the dream had more detail than ever before. She'd heard her mother's voice as clearly as if LaVita had been there in the dank cell with her.

Inhaling, she caught her mother's scent, and a memory flashed: LaVita, barefooted, scaling the side of the neighbor's old haybarn and disappearing into the loft window. Herself crouched in the pasture, watching, listening. That horrible scream! Her mother's distorted voice—*God, how could she have forgotten?*

Her sweat turned cold and she clamped her teeth to stop their chattering.

The four figures weren't just a nightmare; they were

real. She had been in the pasture that night and had seen her father's killers. But they remained faceless phantoms. Had she seen their faces? Did she know, somewhere in her subconscious, who they were?

Another memory flashed before her, one that for some reason she'd never lost—her father's funeral. Only Martha and Monkey and Thelma Patterson had gone with her to bury him in the Tetumka cemetery.

Chantalene dragged herself to the toilet, clutching the blanket around her. Dry heaves wrenched her empty stomach. When the spasms stopped, she rinsed her face and hands beneath the lime-caked faucet, then drank from her hands.

Lying on the cot again, watching the striped square of window lighten toward morning, she asked herself a pivotal question:

*Why keep fighting it?*

She couldn't name one thing about her life that made it worth saving.

But she had no gun, no pills, not even a belt. And if she gave up, *they* got away with murder. She was too damned mad to die.

# EIGHT

At dawn, a ray of sun knifed through the glassless east window of his parents' abandoned farmhouse and targeted Drew Sander's right eye. The scent of musty carpet beneath his sleeping bag on the living room floor mixed with the clean chill of country morning air. He'd gone to sleep on top of the bag wearing only his skivvies, but sometime during the night he had scrambled inside.

Quickly, he pulled on yesterday's jeans and a clean t-shirt and socks from his duffle bag. For breakfast, he reached for a cigarette, checked that impulse, and fished a lukewarm cola from his grocery bag. Any source of caffeine in a pinch.

Barefoot, he stepped out the front door and surveyed the quiet morning. He couldn't help but smile. How long had it been since he'd had more than a mile of space between him and the nearest human? It felt pretty damned good. For a moment he thought of Emily, at this hour deep in REM sleep in their Manhattan apartment.

Too much thinking. If he was going to get this old house ready to sell, he had a lot of work ahead of him.

Drew finished the cola and found his sneakers, then set to work ripping up stained carpet. The dust made him sneeze. Yesterday evening he had pried the boards off the outside of the downstairs windows—possibly a mistake since most of the glass was broken—and he'd got the electric pump going on the well. He had plenty of fresh water in the house, all of it cold. The pump was on a separate line from the electricity to the house, though, and the power wasn't getting through in here. He'd have to find an electrician to deal with that; he didn't do electricity.

Monkey had warned him the house was a mess and said he was welcome to spend the night with them. But last night he'd felt too hot and tired to go to the Jenkses' for supper. Instead he'd opted for Vienna sausages and pork and beans straight from the cans. Most of all, he hadn't wanted to discuss that murder scene over dinner. If he didn't think about it, maybe the whole ugly episode—along with the gnawing memory of Chantalene Morrell's forlorn face—would just go away.

Pulling up the carpet was dirty, throat-choking work, but underneath he found hardwood floors that city folk would die for the chance to refinish. He'd forgotten about those floors, though he vaguely remembered his mother's pride when they finally bought carpeting. When you had to wax and polish by hand, he supposed, wood floors lost their appeal.

After piling the carpet outside in the yard, he swept the remaining dirt from the living room and swabbed cobwebs from the ceilings and walls, whistling while he worked. He worked deliberately, taking his time. There was no telephone to ring, no deadlines to meet. A meadowlark's song floated through the open windows and he felt his nervous system unknotting.

At mid-morning he recognized the roar of Monkey Jenks' pickup and went out to greet him.

"You been busy," the farmer drawled, eyeing the house and rolls of dirty carpeting.

Drew smiled. "Physical labor feels good for a change."

"Thought you might like to borrow these." Monkey

bobbed his head toward a lawn mower and ladder in his truck bed.

"They're exactly what I need." Which, of course, Monkey had known. They hoisted the hardware out of the truck and Monkey handed him a red plastic jug of gasoline. "I sure appreciate this," Drew said.

They moved across the driveway to the shade of an elm tree, where they could face the house and assess the project Drew had undertaken. It was going to be one of those spectacular Indian summer days, Drew noted, not quite as hot as yesterday, but clear and bright as a child's imagination.

Monkey squatted with one knee slightly above the other for balance, his elbows propped on each leg, as farmers hereabouts always did when they talked. Drew had seen his father and Monkey spend an hour at a time in this position, discussing crops and weather, with long silences between. One of them would pick up a stick and draw squares in the dust; the other would squint toward some distant spot on the horizon, his eyes shaded beneath a weathered hat. Questions both insignificant and cataclysmic were analyzed and settled that same way.

In the etiquette Drew was born to, Monkey's stance conferred upon him the rank of an equal. He reciprocated by squatting as best he could. Monkey picked up a twig; Drew squinted.

"Sorry I can't stay and provide some elbow grease," Monkey said. "Got to drive to OK City today and try to buy some heifers while the market's down." He called it "oak city," but Drew knew he meant Oklahoma City. Monkey had on his good jeans and clean hat in honor of his visit to the state capital.

"I'd like to do this myself, anyway," Drew said, and Monkey nodded his understanding. "But can you recommend an electrician?"

"Best hand with that would be Thelma Patterson, unless you want to wait a week for somebody from El Rio to come out."

*"Thelma?"* Drew felt a glimmer of guilt for his gender stereotyping, but Monkey didn't notice. "The same Thelma Patterson that used to knit baby booties for every newborn in Opalata County?"

"Same one. Martha says Thelma's moved up to baby *af-ghans* now." Monkey accented both syllables. Beneath the hat brim, his blue eyes glittered. "Ya gotta admire somebody who can knit up a hound."

Drew laughed aloud, and Monkey wheezed his Deputy Dog chuckle.

"Thelma's the postmistress, too," Monkey added. "Plus she sort of fills in for the lack of a local newspaper."

"A woman of many talents," Drew said, still smiling. He remembered Thelma as a few years younger than his mother, and loquacious in a harmless way. "I'll ask her to come out and check the wiring."

"I could swing by the post office and mention it to her, if you like."

"Perfect. Ask her to come this afternoon if she can."

Monkey stood, his knees cracking with the stiffness of waning middle age.

*If Dad were still alive,* Drew thought, *he'd be Monkey's age. I wonder if he'd have mellowed.*

"Thanks for coming by."

Monkey climbed into his truck, waved, and drove away in a cloud of dust.

Thelma Patterson arrived at one o'clock. Drew noted that if he ever needed anything from the Tetumka post office, he'd better get to the window before noon.

A short, plump woman with brown hair and an Avon-pink smile, Thelma hailed Drew as if they were old pals.

"Drew Sander! Home at last. Is it permanent this time?" Her curious eyes flicked over him like a stockman assessing cattle.

He kept his answer vague. "Can't say for sure, Thelma. But I do need to get some juice to the house. I'm too citified to live without electricity." He gave her his most charming smile.

"Aren't we all?" she said, laughing. "To hell with the good old days."

Thelma strapped a tool belt over her jumpsuit and cheerfully wiggled into spaces half her size, checking for faulty wiring. By three, she'd found the problem, set about splicing wires, and filled Drew in on a decade and a half of Tetumka gossip. He responded with appreciative comments as he watched Thelma test outlets. "Is that right? ... You don't say."

Her husband Billy Ray had left Tetumka twenty-some years ago to seek better employment, but she'd refused to leave her hometown. "He wrote me once and then disappeared," she said, still sounding surprised after all these years. "I never heard from him again."

He also learned that Opal Bond had gone hysterical and taken to her bed when she found out about her husband's murder. Little Willie, by contrast, ranted and threatened revenge, but everybody figured he was too scared to make good on his threats. Big Willie's funeral was set for tomorrow and the procession would pass right by Drew's house on its way to the Tetumka Cemetery.

Thelma was skillful at her work, and not just the wiring. Every few stories, she asked him an off-hand question or two, and before he realized he'd said anything, she knew he'd married a New Yorker, had no kids, and was getting divorced. His history would be among the litany of stories at her next stop.

But that was only fair, he supposed, since he hadn't resisted hearing all the neighbors' business and was, in fact, waiting with some interest for her to get around to a particular one.

Thelma replaced fuses and kept talking.

"The Reverend Graves will conduct Willie Bond's service, even though the Bonds never darkened the door of his church. The Reverend's a reformed drinker, you know, a truly compassionate man. He and Laura, that's his wife, have a whole passel of kids. The third youngest had a lot of trouble in school until they discovered she was dyslexic … ."

And Thelma sure hoped Chantalene Morrell had sense enough not to show up at Big Willie's funeral.

*Bingo.*

"Why shouldn't she?" Drew asked, casual as an old shirt.

"Good heavens, Little Willie and Opal are accusing her of the murder!" Thelma said, while they put new light bulbs in all the fixtures. "Lord knows the poor girl had motive; Big Willie tried more than once to get a handful of her, if you know what I mean, not to mention any connection to her daddy's hanging."

"Her *what?* I thought her father committed suicide." He saw Thelma's quick eyes store away his sudden interest.

"Chantalene never believed that story for a minute," she confided. "Swears the suicide note was a forgery." Thelma threw a breaker and lights came on in the house. She smiled with satisfaction. "All finished."

But she had him and she knew it. She waited and made him ask. "Why does Chantalene think the note was phony?"

Thelma leaned forward with a conspiratorial smile. "Because Clyde Morrell could neither read nor write."

They sat on the bumper of Thelma's pickup and shared iced tea from her Coleman jug. Drew furnished the paper cups.

"You mean your daddy never told you about Clyde Morrell?" Thelma asked.

"Not that I remember."

"Well, Matt never was one to carry tales," she said, her voice forgiving. "Besides, it happened twelve years ago, and you were away at college."

Twelve years ago, he thought, would have been about the time of his worst arguments with his dad. Matt had wanted—expected—Drew to take over the farm. During that same time, his father's drinking got worse and his mother was diagnosed with cancer. His dad would barely speak to him then, let alone tell him community gossip.

Unlike Thelma. But like a good newswoman, Thelma didn't editorialize, much. She just reported the facts.

"Clyde Morrell was found hanged. In his pocket was a hand-printed note that said, 'FORGIV ME', with the E left off *forgive,* and signed with his initials, 'C.M.'. Townsfolk took it to be his confession for the rape of Berta Jean Bond, and figured the guilt drove him to take his own life."

"Berta Jean is Big Willie's daughter?" Drew couldn't keep the shock from his voice. In all the years he'd lived here, nothing out of the ordinary had ever happened. Or so he thought. But after he left, apparently, lust and violence had bloomed like wild thistle.

"That's right," Thelma said. "Berta Jean—her real name's Roberta—was the only girl among four brothers, and she never was right. The doctor said brain damage at birth."

Thelma shook her head and tisked. “Poor Opal Bond. It’s no wonder if she’s one egg short of a dozen. Putting up with all those yahoos and her only daughter not even able to take care of herself, let alone help out.”

Drew judged the *yahoos* to be Big Willie and the four sons Monkey Jenks had mentioned.

“One evening Opal went to a revival meeting at the church—the last time anybody’s seen her off the place alone, as a matter of fact—and left Little Willie to look after his sister. The older boys were grown and gone by then, and Berta Jean was thirteen. Had the body of a woman and the mind of a three-year-old child.

“Instead of babysitting, Little Willie went carousing with his friends and left Berta Jean alone. When Opal came home that night, she found the girl bruised up and hysterical, and she’d been raped. Opal called Big Willie, who was still down at the store doin’ books that night, and he called in a doctor from El Rio. While they were waiting for the doc, some of the neighbors gathered at the Bond place to try and help out, and to keep Big Willie under control. He was ranting and swearing revenge.”

In the tradition of expert storytellers, Thelma’s voice dropped to a whisper, forcing Drew to lean toward her.

“Close to midnight, Clyde Morrell came driving past the Bonds’ house, half liquored up,” she continued. “Clyde saw all the lights on and extra cars parked in the yard, so he stopped in to see what all the commotion was about. When Berta Jean got a glimpse of him, she waxed hysterical, shrieking like a banshee, and she wouldn’t let up. Appeared like she was terrified of Clyde Morrell.”

Drew jumped when she hit the word *shrieking* with demonstrative force, and he saw the flicker of success in her eyes.

Now her voice became business-like. “Well, the local

fellas never had much use for Clyde anyway, and that was enough evidence for them. They took Clyde into custody and hauled him to the El Rio jail.

"From the start, Clyde swore it was a case of mistaken identity. Said he'd been playing poker with some guys at a beer joint in the next county. Sure enough, at his trial, three of those old boys showed up and testified he'd been with 'em all evening. And, of course, Berta Jean couldn't identify anybody. Clyde was acquitted, but some folks still thought he was guilty."

"Why would he have stopped at the Bond's house that night, if he was guilty?" Drew said.

Thelma shrugged. "That's a point. Anyway, when they announced the verdict, Big Willie stood up in the courtroom and swore at everybody within earshot, including the judge. They had to put him in the slammer overnight to calm him down. Opal didn't attend the trial; she was home tending to Berta Jean, who'd lost what little mind she had, after the attack.

"Eventually Big Willie put Berta in a home, though Opal fought it. Willie said worrying about that girl was killing Opal and he forbade her even to visit. Opal said he just wanted her free to take care of *him*. She's been bitter as a settin' hen ever since."

Thelma paused to drain her cup of iced tea. Gossip was a thirsty business.

"Couldn't she visit her daughter anyway, even if Willie didn't approve?" Drew asked.

"If she didn't mind gettin' knocked around when he found out."

"Nice guy."

"Oh, Big Willie was a prince. There may be a crowd at his funeral tomorrow, but there won't be many *mourners*."

"I still don't see enough evidence for Mrs. Bond and Little Willie to accuse Chantalene of killing him," he said.

Thelma wagged her head. "She sort of set herself up for it. Ever since she moved back to Tetumka—"

"Back from where?" he interrupted.

"From college. She spent a couple years over at East Central in Ada. On scholarship, as a matter of fact. Anyway, she let people know she thought her father was murdered, and she aimed to see the killers brought to justice. Then the day before Big Willie was killed, she announced that she knew who did it." Thelma raised her eyebrows. "Come to think of it, Chantalene never defined her idea of justice."

A strange feeling started at Drew's hairline and ran down his shoulder blades. His mind retrieved an image of Willie Bond spread-eagled on the wood floor of his grocery with bright red where his face should have been. He also recalled the bone-white face of Chantalene Morrell as she ran out of Bond's Market ... that frame of wild black hair ... those wide, otherworldly eyes that defied forgetting. Was Chantalene Morrell a courageous orphan determined to unravel the riddle of her father's death, or a deceptively beautiful sociopath?

Sitting on the front step of her tiny, paintless house yesterday while she talked to Monkey, she hadn't fit either profile. She'd just looked miserable—and *tired.*

He felt Thelma watching him. "So what do I owe you for the electrical work?" he said quickly, tossing his ice cubes on the grass in a gesture of termination. "I hope you'll take an out-of-state check."

"I certainly won't."

When he looked startled, Thelma smiled and patted his arm. "I'm happy to help you out. Matt and Rose were good friends of mine, and I still miss 'em."

Her eyes were sincere, and it went straight through him. His nose burned. "Me, too. Thanks, Thelma."

He felt like a dope, but he couldn't find anything else to say.

When Thelma had gone, Drew wandered through the house, trying to decide what to do next and fighting a groundless melancholy. He pictured the country cemetery a mile down the road, where his parents were buried. Among the tombstones that angled like an old man's snaggled teeth, an open grave waited for a man nobody would mourn.

If I were making that trip tomorrow instead of Big Willie, he wondered, would anybody mourn for me?

He suddenly felt lonesome for Roosevelt's Bar and Grill on Sixty-Seventh Street, where about this time of day he could suck up beer and nachos and blaspheme whatever team was demolishing the Mets on ESPN. He longed for a place so crowded nobody would talk to him. In New York, a man could get comfortable with his isolation.

But at five o'clock in Tetumka, no such place lay within a day's drive.

He settled for making a list of things to get in El Rio the next day. Measuring the windows for panes of glass, he jotted the specs on his list, along with *get phone connected, ice chest, and beer.* Plenty of beer.

That evening he sat outdoors atop the propane tank and watched a sunset even more spectacular than the night before. Then he went inside, stretched out on his sleeping bag, and dreamed of peeking from the shadows of empty rooms while Willie Bond's funeral procession rolled past his house toward eternity.

The next morning, he decided to get out of there before the dream could come true.

The day was another beauty, with the cottonwoods along the road to El Rio rippling brilliant yellow leaves in the wind. By the time he arrived in the county seat, a few thunderheads crouched on the far western horizon. He knew the farmers needed rain, but he hoped it didn't happen before he could cover his gaping windows.

He stopped first at the builders' supply store for paint and tools, and to leave the window measurements. Modern marketing had reached El Rio; a clerk named Pete promised his "glasses" within an hour. With the back seat of the Volvo laid flat the panes would fit, and Pete would supply foam packing to insulate against the jolts of country roads.

Drew left the store whistling.

He checked on phone service at the local Southwestern Bell Telephone office and browsed through Wal-Mart for half an hour, picking up supplies and work clothes. Not wanting to buy ice and groceries until he was ready to drive home, and with time to kill, he strolled across the town square to the courthouse.

Wouldn't hurt to check that the deed to the farm had been properly recorded in his name after the estate was settled and he'd bought out his sisters' shares. Liz and Janie both lived in California now and had no interest in the home place. If he did decide to sell the house, the abstract would have to be updated, and sometimes these small town clerks didn't get around to posting property changes until someone complained.

The footstone of the Opalata County Courthouse said 1915, only eight years after statehood. Gray limestone stretched up three stories, with bars on the top floor windows marking the location of the county jail. A wide lawn sprinkled with dandelions and towering oak trees surrounded the structure.

Drew descended a flight of stairs to the library of county records, where a musty basement scent combined with that of old books. He loved that smell. Poking through dusty ledgers of land transactions, he was in his element.

In New York he had passed the bar but wound up in the accounting department of his father-in-law's holding corporation, where he supervised tax dodges and became increasingly alarmed about some of the actions required of him. The smell of old paper and the feel of thick book spines in his hands reminded him pleasantly of law school, when he was young and ambitious and uncorrupted.

Before he found the entry he was looking for, though, he overheard a conversation that changed his whole morning and compelled him to perform only the second impulsive act of his life. The first one was marrying Emily, which, he reflected later, should have been a warning.

"They brought in a suspect in that murder over in Tetumka," one of the clerks was telling another, whose desk guarded the entrance and exit to the library. "A woman."

"Bet it's his wife," her co-worker said. "No jury would convict her."

The first clerk, apparently on break from whatever duties she performed upstairs, dug in a tapestry purse the size of a small suitcase and came up with a package of Juicy Fruit gum.

"Nope," she said, offering her friend the pack as an afterthought. "Some sweet young thing with a funny name. Chantalene Morrell."

What else could he do? He went upstairs to set her free.

# NINE

Chantalene glanced up from the tattered magazine. Old Ned, the jailer, was ambling toward her cell, his footsteps scraping on the metal floor. Maybe the lone technician qualified to administer polygraphs had finally shown up for work. Yesterday he was on sick leave, according to Sheriff Justin.

A purple birthmark blotched the elderly jailer's temple and spilled over one ear, and his chronic wretched breath hinted at some unspeakable malady. But he had been kind enough to lend Chantalene his six-month-old copy of *Rod and Gun.*

Old Ned unlocked her cell door. "You're free to go, missy." His nasal voice sounded as surprised as she was. "Some guy's waiting for you."

Chantalene froze. "Some guy?"

She couldn't think of a soul who would take her side in public, let alone bail her out. Much as she hated that urine-scented cell, it suddenly felt safe compared to what might be waiting for her outside.

The jailer jerked his head toward the exit. "You coming, or you want to spend another night with me?" His grin showed an unmatched set of tobacco-stained teeth.

Chantalene dropped the magazine and fled the cell.

Her palms were damp as she signed for her personal possessions—her driver's license and two dollars—and followed Bobby the Deputy down the long hall to Sheriff Justin's office. He tapped on the door, opened it for her, and stood aside, his mission completed. Her skin felt tingly, as if someone had rubbed a balloon across it and electrified her body hair. She took a deep breath and stepped into the room.

Drew Sander lounged in a wooden chair across the desk from Sheriff Justin, a cup of coffee in his hand.

*Drew Sander?*

His long legs crossed in a wide triangle that revealed colored socks and expensive burgundy loafers. He was smiling and shooting the breeze with the sheriff like an old war buddy.

*Who could be frightened of such a yuppie?* Instead, the sight of him—all cool and politicky while she was fresh from two nights in the slammer—pissed her off royally. Who did he think he was?

She could think of only two reasons Drew Sander would come to her aid. Either somebody had put him up to it, or he was a sexist busybody who pictured himself as a white knight. She didn't like one reason any better than the other.

Still, out of jail was out of jail. So she took a deep breath and smiled. "I don't know why you're here, but thanks," she said, and offered her hand. His palm was dry and his grip firm, raising him a notch in her estimation.

"No problem," he said, and lost the notch. She never trusted anybody who said "trust me" or "no problem."

Blond-haired, blue-eyed, the guy was a cliché from a menswear ad. His cotton pants and shirt looked rumpled in that clean-cut, avant garde sort of way. *Give me a break.* By contrast, after two days in the same clothes, her own rumpled look wasn't affected. Her hair felt like a string mop and her mouth like street slime.

She caught the sheriff's gray eyes shifting from her to Sander and back, looking for some connection between them. *If you can find one, Sheriff, you're a better man than I am.*

Or maybe he knew something she didn't. Maybe he'd asked Sander to babysit her.

"Did you post bond, or what?" she asked Sander, dropping the frozen smile. "I'll pay you back, but it may take a while."

"There is no bail for a capital offense in Oklahoma," he said. "If you've been charged. But with no official charges filed, they can't hold you unless you consent."

"Is that a fact?" She turned to Sheriff Justin and her voice rose. "Funny nobody explained that to me." She'd assumed she *had* been charged, and he'd taken advantage of her ignorance.

The sheriff was unruffled. "I considered her a material witness," he said, as if she weren't in the room. Then, to her, "I'll call you when the polygraph guy gets back."

Sander unfolded himself from the chair and stepped between her and the sheriff. "Come on," he said. "I'll give you a ride home." He held the door open.

With one last glare at the sheriff, she left his office and Sander followed. They walked out of the courthouse together, drawing curious glances from the locals. She fought the urge to flip them off. In truth, though, she and Drew Sander must have made a peculiar pair—Mr. Clean and Ms. Offensive. In a cartoon, little wrinkly lines would be rising from her body. She couldn't wait to get home and scrub in a hot shower. No. A bubble bath, as deep as the tub would hold. And wash her hair ... .

But first Drew Sander had shopping to do.

She waited in his car, fighting for patience while he picked up windowpanes and stopped at the Piggly Wiggly for groceries. Thunderheads piled up in the west and the air felt sultry and was hard to breathe. While she sat steaming, she wondered again why Sander suddenly showed up in Tetumka. Her stomach growled and a headache gnawed at her eyeballs.

At last he came out of the grocery store, then spent ten minutes juggling parcels in the back of the car. Finally he came around to her open window and handed her a sack. "You'll have to put this one by your feet."

"*No problem,*" she said, gritting scummy teeth. The sack was heavy with canned goods and fruit juice.

Suddenly he noticed the sky and his eyes widened. "Damn. I've got to get home fast."

Thank God, she thought. He hopped in and they were off.

Chantalene waited until they'd passed the city limits and were zipping along the two-lane blacktop road that impersonated a state highway. Then she tried the direct approach.

"So why did you do it?"

He kept casting nervous glances at the clouds. "Do what?"

Was he dense, or simply one of those men who loved to make communication difficult? "Come to the defense of a murder suspect," she said patiently. "Or do you do that in every small town you pass through?"

He made an effort to bring his attention inside the car. "I'm not sure. Maybe a feeling that outsiders around here better stick together. Besides, I just couldn't picture you burying that meat saw in Willie Bond's forehead."

She snorted. "Then you don't have a very good imagination."

*"You killed him?"* His foot clamped the brake and he looked at her with horror in his eyes.

The car drifted across the centerline. Chantalene pointed toward an oncoming car and he tugged the wheel to the right.

"No," she said. "But Willie was a world-class horse's ass."

His face relaxed and he steadied the wheel. "So I've heard. Any idea who did him in?"

That question was too complicated to answer, especially to a stranger. "Who knows?" She shrugged, and changed the subject. "What did you tell Sheriff Justin?"

"About what?"

"About why you got me out," she said, pronouncing each word deliberately.

"Oh." He flashed a grin full of white teeth that stopped her breath for an unexpected moment. With that tanned face and tiny cleft in his chin, Drew Sander could be extremely attractive, if he were her type.

"I told him I was your attorney," he said.

"You're a lawyer?"

"Sort of."

"How can you be sort of a lawyer?"

"I'm a tax attorney in New York. I've never handled a criminal case, and I'm not licensed in Oklahoma." He shrugged and grinned at her again. "I didn't think the sheriff needed to know all that today."

She had to smile. "Swell. I could have used a real lawyer."

"They'll appoint you one if you're arraigned."

"Right. The public defender's about ninety-five and couldn't hear a cannon in a closed room."

Another flash of white teeth. "Old Jake Waylon's still alive, is he?"

My god, Chantalene thought, he's a thirty-something Good Old Boy.

"Well, they can't have much evidence against you," he added.

She laughed, but without humor. "Only motive and opportunity. People have been convicted with less."

"I can testify there was no blood on your hands or clothes when you came out of the store, if that helps."

She examined his profile, backlit against the car window. "He's observant," she said aloud.

He kept his eyes on the road. "You make an indelible first impression."

Sprinkles dotted the windshield and he frowned, either at the rain or her first impression, she wasn't sure which.

"Red blouse, black jeans, no belt," he recited. "Leather sandals. Two rings on the right hand, none on the left; no fingernail polish. Small, gold hoop earrings, no makeup except lipstick, dark red."

She blinked. "That's creepy." What did she really know about this guy she'd climbed into the car with? Involuntarily, her right hand moved to the door handle.

He noticed that, too. "Relax. I'm harmless," he said. His tone sounded ironic.

"Oh. That's too bad."

He glanced at her, his ears reddening. "Not *that* harmless," he snapped.

"Hey, it's none of my business."

"You can be very annoying, you know that?"

A brilliant flash of lightning interrupted the conversation, followed by a crack of thunder that made them both jump. In the next instant, the sky unleashed a torrent of rain, obscuring the road.

He fumbled for the wiper switch and the headlights. "*Damn* it."

"You afraid of thunderstorms?"

"No, I'm not afraid of thunderstorms," he said irritably.

"I grew up here, too, remember?" A gust of wind rocked the car. "The windows of my house are broken out and now the floors will get soaked."

They drove through the storm in silence. He gripped the wheel with tanned hands Chantalene thought looked more like a farmer's than a lawyer's, except for smooth, clean fingernails. She always noticed hands. His had long, sturdy fingers and golden fuzz that stood up like a halo on the backs of his wrists.

*Quit that,* she told herself. *You've got enough time bombs in your life. You can't possibly add another until one of them expires.*

But then, Big Willie *had* expired, hadn't he?

Drew Sander leaned forward as he drove, peering through the heavy rain. She centered her breathing and relaxed, waiting. In a moment she began to perceive his aura, a pale yellow light that pulsed next to his skin, fringed with blue at the perimeter. Mixed signals. Indecisive. She wondered whether that was an indication of his basic personality, or just his reaction toward her.

She looked across the space between them again. His body language said *leave me alone,* but she couldn't do it.

"Why did you come back here?" she asked.

He took a long time answering. "My excuse was to fix up the home place for sale." He exhaled, the irritation gone from his voice.

"But that wasn't the real reason," she said, finishing his implication.

"I wanted to get away from New York for a while."

Rain and wind battered the car, but inside Chantalene felt unaccountably safe and dry. She didn't ask him to tell her why he'd left New York; she just waited.

"It sounds corny," he said finally, "but I feel as if I've had three lives. One here, growing up on the farm. Another in college and law school, where I was responsible for nobody but me—a selfish and happy time. Then a third life in New York, where I went to work in a close-knit family business and married the boss' daughter."

"Wow," she said.

He smiled and shook his head. "What a cliché, huh? The job pays great, but it feels dirty. And the job and the marriage seem tied together; I can't get out of one without affecting the other." His ears reddened again. "That's more than you wanted to know, I'm sure."

"Actually, you've made me feel better. Misery loves company."

"Maybe that's why I got you out of jail. I thought you could use some help."

"And I'm not appropriately grateful." She sighed. "Look, just so we understand each other, I've been looking out for myself since I was twelve, and I'm used to it. I appreciate what you did today, really, but I don't need or expect any help."

"Fine," he said, without looking at her. She saw a tiny muscle tighten in his jaw, a sure signal she'd offended his ego. By mutual consent, they fell silent.

The rain slackened when they neared Tetumka. "There's a short cut to my place coming up," she said, "but it may be too muddy."

He nodded. "I know the road, but I don't have four-wheel drive. I'd better stick to the blacktop as far as I can."

Rain and fatigue mellowed her mood, and she felt a twinge of regret for biting the hand that freed her. Then, too, she liked the way his eyebrows wriggled together like caterpillars when he frowned.

"After I bathe and change, I could come over and help you mop up rainwater and install windowpanes," she said. "I've had lots of practice at mothering an old house."

"That's okay," he said. "I have nothing else to do."

*Ah, yes. If I don't want your help, you don't want mine.* "Nothing except drink all that beer you put in the ice chest, and feel sorry for yourself?"

He shot her a look. "No wonder you have so many friends in this town," he said.

She guessed she deserved that.

The rain eased to sprinkles by the time they turned down the road to her place. Patches of blue showed behind the clouds.

"Better let me out at the road," she suggested. "My driveway is a loblolly after a rain like this."

He pulled over in the track beside her mailbox and she crawled out of his car, leaning down to look at him before shutting the door.

"I still don't understand why you did this," she said, "but thanks. I owe you."

"No you don't," he said. "Unless you skip town and make me look like an accessory. Then I'll hunt you down like a dog."

She lifted her eyebrows. "That might be fun."

He laughed, an open, genuine sound. She shut the door and stepped back from the car. *He should laugh more often.*

Preoccupied, she hadn't noticed another vehicle approaching.

Martha Jenks' green Buick pulled up alongside. Her face peered out the open window, creased with unconcealed worry. "Thank goodness, you're back. I couldn't believe it when Monkey told me the sheriff had kept you up there. I came over to feed your animals."

Martha ducked her head and waved at Drew. "Drew Sander! I expected you for supper last night. Lands, if you don't look just like your daddy! Good to see you."

"Good to see you, too," Drew said. He looked embarrassed and Chantalene wondered why.

Martha turned back to her. "Are you okay?"

"I'm fine, Martha. Drew gave me a ride home."

"I want you both at my supper table tonight, and no arguments, you hear? Six-thirty sharp. I'll bet neither of you has eaten a decent meal in days."

"You don't have to twist *my* arm," Drew said.

"Good. You can bring Chantalene, then. She doesn't have a car. See you both this evening." Martha's eyes made an assessing glance from Chantalene to Drew and back again before she waved and gunned the big Buick down the muddy road.

The Mother of the World strikes again. Chantalene watched both cars pull away. She ought to feel grateful, she supposed, but instead she felt manipulated. A social occasion underpinned with abundant advice from her former foster-mother was the last thing she wanted tonight. Why didn't she have the spine to refuse?

She knew why, of course. She wanted to see Drew Sander again. She told herself it was because she wasn't sure she could trust him.

# TEN

The damp wind that followed the rain felt more like spring than autumn. Chantalene and Drew rode the three miles to Martha and Monkey Jenks' place without talking, the windows of Drew's car open to the breeze. She saw him examine each newly sown wheat field they passed, assessing them with a farmer's eye. He belongs here, she thought, and he doesn't even know it. An odd disappointment caught in her chest. Or maybe it was envy.

The Jenkses' vintage two-story farmhouse presided over their farm. Permanent white siding—the kind you never have to paint—updated the second story of the house, and brick veneer girded the first. Tubs of bright geraniums dotted the porch and green lawn, which was protected from marauding livestock by chain-link fencing and a white wooden gate. Newly washed by rain, the house gleamed in late afternoon sunlight.

"Wow," Drew commented, parking the Volvo in front of the gate.

"I know. It makes my place look like a share-cropper's shack," Chantalene said.

"Makes me realize how much work I have left on my folks' house."

Chantalene gave a half-smile. "I did that same thing when I moved back."

"What?"

"Kept calling it my folks' house instead of mine."

"I haven't moved back," he corrected, perhaps too quickly. "The house is for sale."

They stepped out onto the gravel driveway, scattering curious white chickens. The outbuildings, too, looked neat and newly painted. A green tractor with a glassed-in cab sat inside the open door of the slant-roofed red barn.

"Look at that," Drew said. "An air-conditioned tractor. Bet it has a radio, too." He smiled. "Monkey always did believe in modern equipment. Unlike my dad."

"Hel-looo, strangers!" Martha called from the front porch.

"I smell fried chicken!" Drew answered.

Martha responded with a smile. "It's all ready. Come in and have some iced tea 'til Monkey gets in from chores."

Martha wore a cotton shirtwaist dress and sensible, white leather shoes. She waited for their approach, wiping already-clean hands on a terry dishtowel. Chantalene remembered the gesture. Whenever Martha was in the house, she carried that towel around like worry beads. Martha was a fusser, a quality Chantalene found both endearing and irritating. Martha had tried so hard to replace her mother, and that was the heart of the tension between them; Chantalene didn't want her mother replaced. She needed Martha as friend, instead.

"Lands, it's good to see the both of you," Martha said as they approached the front porch.

Martha met Chantalene's eyes, and the look of naked concern Chantalene saw there cut through her. She squeezed her hostess' outstretched hands and smiled, thankful Martha wasn't given to hugging. "You're looking great."

"And you're skinny as a fence rail. We'll have to feed you better."

Martha was one of those rare tall women who are unafraid of their height, her posture straight as a silo. Chantalene admired that. The few pounds Martha had put on during middle age softened her large bone structure and kept the lines from her face. As a young woman, she must have been impressive, in the way people call *handsome* instead of pretty. Nearing sixty, Martha's tanned face and hazel eyes still looked young, her arms firm and strong.

In fact, there was much about Martha to admire. But as a girl, whenever Chantalene had begun to feel affection for Martha, she'd suffered a backlash of guilt, as if she were being disloyal to her real mother's memory. Understanding that, she hoped to be able to get past it now.

"Thanks for inviting me," Drew said as they followed Martha into the house. "I sure dreaded facing another can of pork and beans."

In the kitchen Martha handed them foggy quart-sized glasses of fresh iced tea. "Sugar, Drew? I know Chantalene takes hers straight."

"Thanks. I'll help myself." Drew added two spoonfuls and dropped a lemon slice into the glass, stirring vigorously. He drank half of it without a breath. "That hits the spot."

Martha looked pleased. "You kids make yourselves at home. I'll just finish the gravy and set the food on."

"Can I help?" Chantalene offered. "I can't make gravy as good as yours, but I could set the table."

Martha shook her head and shooed them toward the dining room. "It's all done. You keep Drew company." She opened an outside door that led from the kitchen toward the barn and yelled loud enough to be heard in the next county. "Mon-KEY! Company's here and I'm making the gravy!"

Chantalene lead Drew into the large living and dining

area, which seemed dark and cool after the bright kitchen, even though Martha wasn't running the air conditioner.

It was the first time Chantalene had been in Martha's house since she'd gone away to college. The furniture, the flowered drapes that bordered two tall windows, open to the breeze, were all familiar. But she couldn't conjure one memory of herself at twelve, newly abandoned to this house. It was as if those years had evaporated from her life. She did remember later years, after the running away, after the foster homes. She had stayed here most of her junior and senior years in high school, and except for the nightmares, she'd been all right. But even that period of her life seemed faraway and unreal, like something she'd read in a book.

Four places were set on the huge mahogany dining table. "I hope you're hungry," Martha called from the kitchen. "I know I am!"

Chantalene heard the refrigerator door opening and closing.

Drew milled toward the far end of the room where an overstuffed sofa and two leather recliners gathered around a TV. He inspected a group of framed, dried wildflowers hung on one wall, hand-labeled by Martha, and the books on a nearby shelf. She wondered if Drew could remember details of his early teens—whether anybody could—but it seemed too personal a question to ask him.

He paused before a fireplace set with gas logs to examine an old-timey, sepia photograph of a man and wife staring down from the mantel. The woman was big-boned and plain, with Martha's eyes and long hair braided into a ring behind her head. The man stood with a hand on her shoulder, dark-eyed and somber.

"That's Martha's mother and father," Chantalene said.

"So I guessed."

Below the man's heavy eyelids, his black eyes skewered the camera with an expression that must have made his children call to mind their sins.

"I'll bet he was hard to lie to," Drew said fervently.

Martha, coming in from the kitchen with a platter in each hand, heard the remark. "That's for sure. But he wasn't above telling a few himself." Her smile didn't quite reach her eyes. She set the bowls on the table and went out again.

"I guess I'm not the only one who had conflicts with his father," Drew whispered.

The aroma from a mountain of country fried chicken now on the table pulled Drew away from the dark-eyed man in the photograph. But Chantalene stood a moment, wondering whether Martha's attempts to mother the world arose from her childhood under the authority of those stern parents. It had never occurred to her before to wonder about Martha's childhood.

Monkey's boots clattered on the kitchen floor and Chantalene turned to smile at him as his shoulders filled up the doorway. His forehead shone white above the eyebrows where his hat had protected it from years in the sun. The rest of his face was brown as leather.

"Evening, folks," he said. "Sorry if I made you wait. I'll wash up right quick."

She'd always felt more relaxed with Monkey than with Martha. Ironically, though Monkey never tried to replace her father, she'd come close to accepting him in that role. The only thing that prevented it, it seemed to her now, was a lack of real conversation between them. He talked easily enough with other farmers; perhaps it was just women folk who stunned him to silence.

Monkey ducked down the hallway toward the bathroom and Martha swept in with three more steaming bowls balanced in her hands. "Come get it while it's hot!"

Drew startled Chantalene by holding her chair and then Martha's before he sat down. Steam curled from pottery bowls of mashed potatoes, cream gravy, and home canned green beans seasoned with bacon and onion. She smelled fried squash, pickled beets, and homemade bread—an orgy for the olfactories.

Drew's face looked absolutely childish with delight. "Thank god country folks don't worry about cholesterol."

"They work it off, unlike lawyers," Chantalene said.

"I'm actually more of a tax accountant ... "

"So you get lots of exercise?"

When Monkey was seated, Drew helped himself to three pieces of chicken and passed the platter to Chantalene. She tensed, knowing Martha would require an explanation of why she passed up the main course. One day during her sophomore year at college, the thought of biting into a former living thing had overwhelmed her, and she hadn't eaten a bite of meat since.

She passed the platter to her left and took too many mashed potatoes to make up for it. For the moment, at least, Martha was busy filling her own plate and hadn't noticed. Drew and Monkey began to discuss the last wheat harvest, which Monkey described as the best in several years.

"Harvest was magic when I was a kid," Drew said. "The summer I was fifteen, I begged Dad to let me sign on with a combine crew that followed the harvest north. I pictured myself cutting a swath through Kansas and the Dakotas all the way to the Canadian border."

"I think you'd have found it wasn't quite that romantic," Martha said.

"No doubt. Anyway, Dad said he needed me to stay and help with plowing. Which wasn't true, really. Only one person could ride the tractor at a time and my sister, Liz, was plenty willing to spell him off. She could plow a furrow as straight as anybody."

"That she could," Monkey said.

Chantalene munched her vegetables quietly, happy to be inconspicuous.

"Dad and I didn't agree on much of anything by that time, though," Drew was saying. "I think he figured if I left with the harvest crew I might keep on going."

"Maybe it was your mom who thought that," Martha pointed out.

Drew shrugged. "Maybe so. And maybe she was right."

"Monkey says you're planning to sell the house. You're not thinking of selling the farm, too, are you?" To a born farmer like Martha, selling land was akin to exposing oneself in public.

"No, not the land," he assured her, then grinned. "And if I did, I'd give you and Monkey first chance at it."

This guy should be in public relations instead of taxes, Chantalene thought.

"Thelma tells me your marriage is on the rocks," Martha said. "Sorry to hear that. Sure happens a lot these days."

Oops. Chantalene couldn't help smiling. *Let's see him shmooze his way out of this one.* She glanced at Monkey, who ignored Martha's remark by concentrating fiercely on his plate. He spent a lot of time ignoring, she remembered.

But Drew was good; he segued right into a new subject. "Could I have some more potatoes, please, Martha? What a shame you don't have a daughter to inherit your country cooking!"

"I wish I did," Martha said evenly, without even a glance in Chantalene's direction as she sent the gravy bowl after the potatoes. "Especially now that I'm old enough to be a grandma. I guess Monkey and I should have adopted."

Drew's spoon froze in mid-air and Chantalene saw his face redden.

"Have some more potatoes, Chantalene," Martha urged, checking her plate. "Didn't you get any chicken?"

Drew saved her by changing subjects again, and she had the feeling it was intentional. Could he be that perceptive?

"Do you still volunteer over at the children's ward in El Rio Hospital?" he asked Martha.

Chantalene scooped out more potatoes under Martha's watchful eye, though she hadn't finished the first helping yet.

"No," Martha said, "I switched to the old folks home a few years ago. They have a harder time finding volunteers, let alone somebody with nurse's training. And it's run by the church, so they're always short on funding."

"I didn't know you were a nurse."

Chantalene looked up, surprised. "Neither did I."

Martha gave a modest shrug. "Just an LPN. I took a class now and again while I was helping out at the hospital, and finally got my certificate. Now all the neighbors call me to help deliver foals or cure some heifer of the bloat."

Drew burst out laughing. Martha looked embarrassed and tapped at her mouth with a napkin. "Sorry. What a thing to say during supper."

"Don't worry," Drew said. "If that scene at Bond's Market didn't permanently spoil my appetite, nothing will."

Chantalene wanted to kick him. But like a clumsy puppy, he probably wouldn't have understood the punishment.

Martha clucked and exchanged a glance with Monkey. "Monkey told me about that. What an awful thing for you to stumble into. You, too, Chantalene."

"Not as bad for me as for Big Willie," she said dryly.

Martha put down her napkin and laid both hands in

her lap. Her tone was deliberate. “Chantalene, I know you couldn’t have done that to Willie Bond, but ... have you considered the fact that you might have caused it to happen?”

Chantalene dropped her fork.

“*Martha ...* ” Monkey said sharply.

She ignored him. “That speech you made at the Selby’s farm! You’ve got the whole town suspicious of each other.”

Monkey’s face turned dark. “Martha ... ”

“They ought to be suspicious,” Chantalene said. Her food had turned to concrete in her stomach. Even Drew stopped eating.

“They didn’t come here for a lecture,” Monkey warned his wife.

“I know, but somebody’s got to talk sense to her.” Her eyes remained fixed on Chantalene. “You can’t accuse folks of something like that and expect not to have consequences.”

“I *don’t* expect not to have consequences,” Chantalene said. “And pardon me for not mourning Big Willie the Lech. I can think of any number of reasons the world’s better off without him. Not the least of which is that he helped murder my father!”

The sound of Monkey’s chair raking back from the table startled them all. His tall form towered over them as he met Martha’s eyes, and Chantalene thought this time he would put a stop to Martha’s meddling. Then a look crossed Martha’s face that Chantalene had never seen before, an expression she couldn’t quite name, and Monkey’s anger dissolved into sorrow. He dropped his napkin in his empty chair and left the room without a word.

Chantalene sat with her mouth open, her breathing stopped. She heard the kitchen door open and slam. She glanced sideways at Drew, but his frown seemed more curious than shocked.

They sat in silence for several moments before Martha cleared her throat and picked up her iced tea. She didn't even apologize. "Drew, let me give you some unsolicited advice," she said, her tone as normal as if nothing had happened. "This girl's like a tornado—best viewed from a distance."

Drew actually smiled. "I figured that out earlier today."

Chantalene turned on him. "You too, Brutus?"

The innocent surprise on his face made her even angrier. He spread his hands, palms up.

"Feel free to stay for dessert," she said. "I'll walk home."

She stood up so fast her chair tipped, but he caught the back before it went over.

"Chantalene, please sit down," Martha said. Her voice sounded tired now. "I'm only worried about you. I'm afraid you're putting yourself in danger."

"I didn't ask you to worry about me and I can't stop you," she said. "But why can't you admit that my father was *lynched* by these people, for god's sake? They wrecked my family, left me an orphan, and nobody cares! Well I do. They'll have to answer for what they've done."

She stormed out of the dining room and down the porch steps with the image of Martha's stone expression and Drew's stunned face burning behind her eyes.

She stopped outside the gate. Monkey's dejected silhouette leaned against the fence beside the barn, staring across a field toward the sinking sun. She knew how he hated conflict, but the scene was Martha's fault, not hers. She hesitated a moment but couldn't find anything to say to him. She turned and strode down the driveway toward the shale road.

She'd walked almost a mile before she heard the car approach slowly behind her. She knew who it was without looking back. She moved to the side of the road where the pebbles were large and rough beneath the thin soles of her sandals. A tiny rock lodged painfully between her toes, but she refused to stop and dislodge it until the car passed.

Which it didn't. For a quarter mile she limped along with Drew's Volvo rolling slowly behind. When she finally stopped to remove the sandal and shake out the stone, his car pulled up at an angle across her path.

He leaned toward the open passenger-side window. "For pete's sake, get in the car. Those sandals won't last another mile."

She glared at him in silence, replacing her shoe.

"I was caught in the middle!" he said. "What did you expect me to say?"

She didn't answer.

"I was just trying not to take sides."

"The hell you were! You sided with her."

"I only agreed that you're like a tornado. Kicking up dust and leaving debris behind."

"That simpering smile won't work on me the way it does on Martha."

"Sorry, I'm out of practice. I've been married for years."

She looked at his infuriating yuppie face. God how she wanted to wipe off that smile. "All right. I'll get in, if you'll go where I tell you."

"To hell?"

She climbed in and slammed the door. "Drive to your place."

His eyebrows rose. She glared straight ahead.

He drove maddeningly slow and turned at the corner that led to his farmhouse. When they neared his driveway he touched the brake.

"Keep going," she ordered. "I want to show you something."

Grudgingly, he removed his foot from the brake and the car rolled on for half a mile. There the road dipped to bisect a low area lined with trees, a place the locals called Animal Draw because of the wildlife it attracted. The land backed up to hers, and Drew's family had owned it for generations.

"Stop here," she said.

He pulled over beside the grader ditch. She got out, crossed the ditch and climbed through the fence. Dried stubs of broomweed gouged her feet. Without looking back, she headed toward the old haybarn, nearly concealed now by cedars and blackjack trees.

She heard him following, but after a minute or two he stopped and made a stand. "Damnit, what are we doing here?"

She turned to face him, shielding the last rays of sun from her eyes with one hand. Random spirals of hair floated around her face like loose spider webs in an updraft.

"I said I want to show you something. I want you to understand why I can't leave this alone."

A Monarch butterfly hovered above a clump of milkweed, settling in for the night. She could feel its fluttering wings in her stomach as she watched Drew's gaze flicker from her to the haybarn behind her. His haybarn. The irritation in his face changed into realization, then to horror.

*"It happened here?"* His voice dissolved in the wind.

So he hadn't known. She stood still a moment, then turned and tramped on through the pasture.

The barn stood gray and silent in the rank grasses, its roofline a sagging A. Along a forgotten path, the bowed heads of sunflowers no longer faced the sun. The relentless wind had stripped the barn of doors and shutters, and weathered shingles had peeled away, exposing rafter bones to baking heat and winter snows.

On the exposed side of the barn, planks swung loose like rotting skin from a skeleton. She pushed one aside and slipped through the gap. Drew's footsteps approached behind her, his body cutting off the light as he wedged inside. He stood beside her facing the center of the barn while their eyes adjusted to the dim interior. The only sound was the moan of the wind through the slotted roof.

The barn had been left undisturbed all these years. She'd come here once during the summer, when her courage to face the past weakened, when the temptation to give up was almost too strong. Now she inhaled the smells of damp earth and rotting wood, and raised her eyes to the weathered rope that hung like a lifeless serpent across the center rafter. Its tail coiled around a vertical support post; its head was a severed noose, swaying faintly in the wind.

She heard the breath go out of him.

"He wasn't much older than you when he died," she said, her throat tight.

Drew made a small, choked sound. She turned toward him.

"I'm sorry," he said. "I'm so sorry."

She had wanted to shock him. But the expression of genuine misery on his face somehow offended her. "It's not *your* fault," she said, frowning.

"No." He met her eyes and his voice sounded strained. "But what if my father was one of the hangmen?"

# ELEVEN

It hadn't occurred to Chantalene to suspect Matt Sander of complicity in her father's murder. Silence followed them back across the darkening pasture, and on the short drive to her house. Drew stopped the car in her driveway but left it running.

"Come inside," she said, and had to repeat it before her words got through to him. He looked at her as if he'd been somewhere far away. Then he nodded and switched off the motor.

They got out and Bones came to sniff the visitor's knees. After that, to Chantalene's amazement, the dog ignored him. Drew sat at her kitchen table staring into space while she heated water for tea and wished she had something stronger.

She set the steaming mugs on the table. He looked at his tea suspiciously and sniffed before he took a sip.

"Pretty good," he said, obviously being polite. "What is it?"

"Herbal tea. Better for you than coffee."

He shook his head. "You're a vegetarian, aren't you? That's the only reason I can think of anybody would pass up country fried chicken."

"Thank goodness Martha isn't as observant as you are," she said.

"Are you a Zen Buddhist, too? Sleep on a bed of nails?"

"When I sleep at all," she said, "it's in a perfectly normal bed. But I do practice meditation."

"And you have a computer, but no TV. Now why would folks around here think you're strange?"

Despite his attempt at humor, his face looked shell-shocked. She leaned her elbows on the table and looked at him. "Why did you say that about your father?"

He let his breath out slowly, frowning. "It's a long story, with a lot of family history in it."

She nodded but said nothing, watching him attentively, leaving it up to him to fill the silence.

He huffed another deep breath. "From the moment I was born, Dad assumed I'd take over the farm someday. My great-granddad homesteaded the land and Dad couldn't imagine a Sander not living on it. I think one of my sisters might have stayed here, if he'd given either of them any encouragement, but he didn't. I was the only son, and he expected me to work the land.

"Even when I went off to college, he thought it was temporary rebellion, that I'd eventually see the light and come home. When I finally told him straight out that I was going to law school and didn't want to farm, he was furious. He actually hit me. And I would have struck back if Mom hadn't intervened. She was always the peacemaker."

His eyes filled and he tipped his head back and contemplated the ceiling. The yuppie cockiness was gone now, and Chantalene could picture him as a boy growing up on the neighboring farm, tied to the land in ways he didn't understand, at odds with a dominant father. It was a side of him she hadn't imagined. She stared into her cup and waited.

"Mom said he'd get over it eventually," Drew went on, "and after a few months Dad and I were at least civil to each other when I came home to visit. Which wasn't often. He had started to drink, and things were never the same."

His hand rested on the table beside his cup, the long fingers still and graceful as a sculpture. A sculpture that invited touch. She squeezed her hands around her tea mug, instead.

"Not long after that," he said, "Mom was diagnosed with cancer. Dad's drinking got even worse and I blamed myself, but maybe that was egocentric. Maybe some other demon drove him to alcoholism."

"Like guilt over a lynching?" she said.

Pain threaded his face. "It all happened about the same time. He never told me Clyde was hanged, let alone in our haybarn."

"That doesn't mean your dad helped do it. The barn is closer to this house than it is to yours, so it was handy. And it's isolated."

"Maybe so," he said.

"Was your dad the vigilante type?"

He paused, thinking it over. "He had a temper that could be brutal. I don't mean he abused us. Aside from a strapping or two when I was a kid, he only hit me that one time, and he never struck my sisters. In fact, he had no tolerance for men who abused women." He met her eyes. "If Dad believed Clyde raped that girl and got away with it, he might have gone right along with vigilante justice. I just don't know."

She shook her head. "If only people had known my dad the way I knew him, they never could believe he was guilty." The unfairness with which the community judged her father still stung.

"Everybody thought he didn't treat your mother right."

"He was jealous, that's all. He loved her fiercely, and I think he was amazed that she'd married him. He always feared losing her. But he never raised a hand to either of us." She sighed. "My father wasn't perfect. He was uneducated and a gambler, but unbelievably softhearted. When I learned to read, he was so proud he held me on his lap and listened for hours. Shortly before he died, I convinced him to let me try to teach him to read, too."

She busied herself pouring more tea. Drew let her refill his cup, but he didn't touch it. "Tell me what you know about the hanging, can you? Any details at all," he said.

And so she told him about her lost memories, the sketchy flashbacks, the nightmares. Everything except the vision of four hooded figures skulking through the mist. That particular image seemed too sinister and bizarre to take the shape of words. She had never talked about it to anyone. *Don't ever tell ... .*

At first it was a relief to spill out some of the fear. She acknowledged the panic attacks, the dread of sleep. But once she stopped talking, the silence of the house loomed over them and she felt self-conscious, exposed. The compassion on his face embarrassed her. She swirled the tea with her spoon.

He seemed to read her discomfort and he looked away, shifted in his chair. "How long did you stay with Martha and Monkey?"

"Until the next summer. About six months, though I don't remember much of that, either. When Mom hadn't come back by then, I ran away to try and find her. I was so naive. I had no idea how complicated the world was. Sheriff Justin brought me back, along with a social worker that talked to the Jenkses. The county declared me an abandoned child and made me a ward of the court. Over the next few years, they placed me in four different foster homes, and each time I ran away."

She glanced up, tried to smile. "I was a real mess. One summer I lived on my own for two months before they found me. I slept outdoors or sometimes in an abandoned barn and bathed in a creek. At night I'd steal vegetables from gardens and eat them raw." She shook her head. "I can barely believe it happened. I must have been a little crazy."

He nodded. "It's no wonder."

"Finally Martha got herself declared an official foster parent so I could stay with them until I finished school. She and the high school guidance counselor wangled me a scholarship to Southeastern. What it didn't cover, I worked off in the cafeteria and took a job slinging pizzas on the weekends."

Chantalene glanced at the kitchen clock. It was after midnight and she was exhausted, but she dreaded sleep and its inevitable hauntings. "Are you hungry? I could make a zucchini pizza."

Drew's smile was sheepish. "I happen to have a homemade cherry pie on the back seat of my car."

She laughed. She could picture Martha insisting he take dessert home with him when he left early. Come tornado, fire, or flood, people had to eat.

"And I happen to have ice cream," she said. "Luckily for you, I have no problem eating dairy products or eggs."

Drew cut the pie and she scooped chocolate chip ice cream on top.

"Umm, umm," Drew said after the first bite. "This has got to be illegal."

"If only I'd paid attention, Martha would have taught me to make crust like this." She had a vision of working with Martha in the kitchen, during her last year with them, when she was 17. For a few short weeks, she'd almost been the daughter Martha wanted. Almost. Another wrinkle of regret for their argument etched through her chest.

She ate every bite of pie and licked her spoon. The kitchen felt cozy in the semi-darkness, with only the small light above the stove burning. Friendly shadows collected in the corners.

Sated on pie, they lingered at the table. Drew talked about the break-up of his marriage, skimming over details. Then he asked a jillion questions about her truck farming operation. Once a farmer, always a farmer, she thought. He may sell that farmhouse, but he'll never let go of the land.

"I'll give you the guided tour during daylight," she promised, then met his eyes. *Had she just invited him to spend the rest of the night?*

She saw the same question in his eyes. And she thought she saw the answer, too—but at that moment Bones set up a ruckus from the front porch.

Between woofs, Chantalene detected the drone of a car coming up her driveway. She looked at Drew and frowned.

He heard it, too, and checked his watch. "You're not expecting anybody, are you?"

"At this hour?"

Quickly she dowsed the light and hurried to the front window in the living room. Drew looked out the window over the kitchen sink.

Peering from behind the curtain, she could see a white pickup pitching over the ruts, without lights, coming fast. An instant of *deja vu* that she couldn't identify stopped her breath.

The pickup swung a wide circle in front of the house, and as it came closer she caught an ominous glint from the driver-side window.

Drew shouted. "Get down!" But she'd already hit the floor.

The front window exploded, showering her with glass. She covered her face with her hands too late and felt tiny, sharp granules against her skin. The echo of a shotgun blast rang in her ears.

The pickup roared away, tires spinning.

Drew was beside her instantly, helping her up. "Are you all right? Careful! Your hair's full of glass."

He led her to the kitchen and picked shards from her hair, dropping them in the sink. She stood still in the darkness, panting, her heart pounding in her ears.

"The son-of-a-bitch," he said. There was fury in his voice. "The lousy chicken-shit son-of-a-bitch! You could have been killed!"

When he'd removed the larger shards, she held her head over the sink and shook it, then shook her shirt.

"I'm all right," she said, feeling for cuts along her arms. She could hear the tremble in her voice. "But remember a few years ago yesterday when I said I don't need any help?"

He nodded.

"I lied."

He held her tightly, and she closed her eyes. They stood that way a long time. She felt his heartbeat against her cheek and smelled his masculine scent and wondered how the night might have turned out without their malevolent visitor.

"I recognized the truck," she said miserably, her eyes still closed. "It was Little Willie Bond."

# TWELVE

Drew spent the night with her, but it sure wasn't the way he'd fantasized it on the short drive from the Jenkses' house earlier that evening.

It was only a few hours before daylight when he finally lay down on the sofa in her living room. The broken window admitted a fresh breeze, along with every sound that inhabited the darkness. Chantalene's old pump shotgun leaned against the armrest beside him, in case of a return visit from Little Willie Bond or some other specter of Tetumka public opinion.

The couch was more comfortable than the sleeping bag on his bare floor at home, but not much. Added to the possibility of being shot at in the night, and to the unsettling image of Chantalene in bed in the next room, the lumpy old sofa was the least of what kept him awake.

What if his father *had* been involved in Clyde Morrell's lynching? Nothing he could do would erase that. He pictured faceless vigilantes bursting through the front door—which opened directly into the living room a few feet from his temporary bed—and he shuddered at the propinquity of evil.

If his father was one of them, it would change his whole point of origin, re-invent his past. And the problem with revisionist history is that, for better or worse, when your past changes, you change, too.

He regretted getting involved in the whole mess. But then he pictured Chantalene's pale face as she sat at the kitchen table and told him her story. At that moment he felt as if he'd known her all his life, probably because they'd grown up only a pasture apart, albeit as strangers. At other moments she seemed unreachable, as baffling to him as she was to her other neighbors.

He twisted on the squeaky sofa, massaging his left arm, which had gone to sleep without him. Bones' toenails clicked across the porch; he wasn't the only one wakeful and nervous.

The murder of Big Willie Bond appeared to hold the key to a riddle that was becoming more and more grotesque. If, presumably, Chantalene didn't kill him, then who did? The wife he'd abused? The son he bullied? Some other member of Clyde Morrell's lynch party, to keep Big Willie quiet? If the sheriff didn't find another suspect, would a jury convict Chantalene on motive and opportunity?

And would they be right?

In the ticking darkness of that haunted house, he lay with his eyes wide open and faced the truth. How much did he really know—or not know—about this woman? He couldn't be positive she hadn't killed Big Willie.

And worse, he was willing to defend her even if she had.

That made him think of Emily, for whom he'd never felt much blind devotion. It was the first time he'd thought of his almost ex-wife in two days. Somehow his wrecked marriage and shady job had shrunk in importance, and that wasn't all bad. But he damned sure didn't need to get entangled with another woman until the mess with Emily was settled.

Nobody returned that night to take pot shots at the house, though Bones set to barking once and nearly gave him heart failure. Shortly before daylight he drifted off to sleep. When he awoke, the room was full of light and he heard Chantalene moving around the kitchen, humming softly.

*Ye gods, a morning person.*

His joints felt stiff, his eyes bleary, and his teeth furry. In her miniature bathroom, he cleaned up as best he could without a toothbrush or razor. In the rational light of day, he looked in the mirror and asked his reflection what exactly he had planned to do if he had to confront a gun-toting Little Willie. Shoot him? He'd never met the guy, but his mental image of Little Willie included extra toes and a lot of banjo picking. The whole scenario was absurd.

He felt foolish and rumpled and grouchy when he dragged himself into the kitchen.

"Morning," Chantalene said, and smiled at him.

She looked as wholesome as a glass of fresh milk. Her long hair was tied loosely at the base of her neck, with a few stray spirals escaping to frame a face that was clear and lovely without makeup. The hem of her over-sized red t-shirt brushed bare tan legs a few inches above the knee. He spent a painful moment feeling jealous of the hem of that shirt.

He tried twice before his voice would work. "Hi. I don't suppose you have coffee?"

"I'm sorry, I don't," she said, her voice sounding truly regretful. "I'll have to buy some."

He liked the implication of that promise.

"Want some strong tea, instead? Or cola?"

He saw her mug of tea on the counter, with a licorice stick as a stirrer. Witches' brew. "Tea will be fine, thanks. Hold the licorice."

She giggled. He sat at the table, his knees cracking.

"Well, I guess Little Willie only wanted to warn us, not kill us," she said cheerfully as she poured his tea.

"Hmmm. Us?"

"Hate by association. You're in Tetumka, remember? I hope your house is still standing."

"That's a happy thought."

She brushed past him, leaving a wake of spice and flowers, and of her own distinctive scent, which reminded him irrationally of a forest floor—damp earth and pine needles. His arms twitched with the impulse to grab her as she walked past, run a hand beneath that t-shirt, rake the stuff off that kitchen table ...

He had to get out of there. Fast. While he still could walk erect.

He stood up. "I'd better go check on it."

She stopped and looked up, an oven mitt on one hand. "Before breakfast?"

Was that disappointment on her face?

"Before Thelma Patterson reports that you had an overnight guest," he said.

Her head tipped back when she laughed. "How provincial of you to worry about my reputation. They only believe I'm a murderer and a witch. Can't have them thinking I'm a *loose woman.*" She laughed again.

"Whatever," he said, feeling the heat on his face. "I really have to go."

He saw on her face the exact moment she figured out why he was in such a hurry. She smiled, her eyes sparkling with amusement.

Women could be so brutal.

He limped toward the front door, past the newly ventilated window. She followed him.

"We'll have to make another trip to El Rio for windowpanes," he said, to divert attention from himself.

"Might as well wait till this is over. Little Willie may be back," she said.

"Ummm." *When, indeed, would it be over?*

She followed him to the car, picking her way around shale rocks in her sandals. The morning was cool and still, the sky a dazzling blue from horizon to horizon without a hint of diesel fumes in the air.

Drew started the engine and turned on the wipers to disperse the dew. He rolled down the window before closing the door, reluctant now to drive away.

Chantalene leaned toward the window. "Thanks for staying over," she said. "It was nice not to be alone."

"No problem."

She stood close to the car, a vague smile on her face, the morning sun silhouetting her features. "Now I owe you double. Maybe I could make dinner for you tomorrow night."

"Sounds good. On one condition."

"What's that?"

"For your own protection, put something on underneath that shirt."

She flushed and clamped her arms around her torso, looking indignant. He couldn't help smiling as he drove away.

His house was still standing, but shards of his two new windowpanes reflected sunlight around jagged, dark holes undoubtedly left by Little Willie's marksmanship.

*The son-of-a-bitch.* Replacing glass in those old wooden windows had been painstaking work, and now he'd get to start all over. He scowled.

Inside, he brushed his teeth, then swept up glass and lead pellets from the living room floor. A robust anger rose up in his throat. He didn't even know this Little Willie character; where did the scumbag get off shooting up his property?

He felt just sleepless and incensed enough to call Little Willie's bluff. He got back in his car and drove to town.

Bond's Market was locked up and dark, the crime-scene tape drooping in yellow waves around the property. He'd have to go into the post office and ask Thelma Patterson how to find the Bonds' house. He regretted that his visit would now be a matter of public record, but then again, it might not be a bad idea if somebody knew where he was headed.

*The last person to see Sander alive was the Tetumka postmistress ...*

He found Thelma perched on a tall stool behind the stamp window. She wore a pink bow in the top of her hair and greeted him with a broad smile.

As always, Thelma was informative. "The Bonds bought the old Radcliff place," she said. "You remember where that is."

He wasn't so redundant as to explain to Thelma why he was going out to the Bonds'. She probably already knew, and if she didn't, she'd find out without his help.

She handed him a thin bundle of mail neatly done up with a rubber band. It hadn't occurred to him that he might have mail. On top was a generic yellow flyer addressed to "Boxholder," so he felt obligated and rented a box. Lucky number thirteen.

In the car again, he looked at the two envelopes beneath the flyer. One came from Wm. Bratten, Emily's attorney, and the other from Emily. The unexpected sight of her familiar handwriting jarred his stomach. He'd deal with that later. He tossed the unopened mail on the floor of his car.

The Bonds lived five miles out of town. He remembered the old Radcliff house as a two-story white frame similar to his parents', but when he drove up, he saw no trace of that old structure. In its place was a sprawling, ranch-style brick residence that might have been pictured in *Western Homes and Gardens.* Big Willie obviously had another source of income besides the grocery.

A small lawn surrounding the house was neatly groomed and flowered, undoubtedly by Opal Bond. But across the driveway, in Willie and Willie's territory, no doubt, the barnyard was a junkman's Mecca. A stack of decaying wooden skids tumbled over beside the paintless barn. Weeds tangled through the rusted skeletons of outdated farm machinery, and all of it was guarded by four of the thinnest, ugliest hounds Drew had ever seen.

His grandmother used to say anybody with more than two dogs was poor white trash.

There was nothing poor or trashy about the house, however. It even had a doorbell. He punched it and waited, bracing for confrontation.

And waited. Finally he realized no vehicles were parked around the place. He'd decided no one was home and turned to go when he caught movement behind one of the window curtains. He rang again. In a moment the door opened wide, revealing a middle-aged woman with a tiny, outdated hat nested on graying brown hair. She held the double handles of a square purse in one hand. Seeing him, her breath sucked in and her eyes widened behind wire-rimmed glasses.

"Mrs. Bond?" he said.

The door closed to a crack. Obviously, she had expected someone else.

"What do you want? I've got a shotgun right here by the door." Her voice was thin and high, scared and contentious at the same time.

He tried to sound reassuring. "I'm Drew Sander. I've come to see Little Willie."

"He ain't home."

"Do you know where I could find him?"

The crack narrowed. "You can't. He's ... gone to the fields. Now go away."

"Please, Mrs. Bond. I don't want to alarm you. But your son shot out my windows last night, and I want to find out why. And give him a chance to pay for them before I file charges," he added sternly.

The last part was a bluff, but it seemed to work. She opened the door an inch wider. "Please don't get him arrested, mister. He's all I got left."

Her watery eyes filled with a different kind of fear, and he felt like a bully. "I'm sorry about your husband's death, Mrs. Bond, but I had nothing to do with it. Little Willie can't go around shooting at everybody."

"What makes you think it was him?" Defensive now; a mother protecting her child.

"Because he shot at Chantalene Morrell's house, too, and she saw him."

The door opened with a jerk. Gone was the meek mama, the subservient wife.

"If you're in league with that devil, *that's* why Willie shot your windows!" she shrieked. "She's a witch, mister, come from bad seed. You'll stay away from her, if you know what's good for you!" Her voice was a high whine, her hands white as eagle talons gripping the doorjamb.

Drew edged backward, in case she really did have a shotgun, and heard the rumble of a pickup turning into the drive. His relief at the distraction melted quickly when he guessed it was Little Willie Bond behind the wheel. Mrs. Bond cringed behind the door again.

The rust-pocked white pickup skidded to a stop in front

of the barn and a slight, wiry man about Drew's age, maybe younger, exploded from the cab and strode across the yard toward them. He wore faded jeans and a plaid flannel shirt with long sleeves, which seemed too warm for the morning. The shirt was untucked and Drew hoped fervently that it didn't conceal a weapon.

Like a rooster fluffing his feathers to make himself appear larger, Drew straightened to his full six-foot height.

"Willie Bond?" he called to the man who was fast approaching.

The glance Little Willie threw at his mother was more threatening than concerned. "Yeah, what do you want?"

His face was red but cleanly shaven, and he had small, hard eyes. Beat-up cowboy boots with extra high heels brought him up to about five-nine.

"I'm Drew Sander—"

"I know who the hell you are." He spat on the ground. "You should be more careful of the company you keep." He stood in front of Drew, feet apart, thumbs tucked into his jeans pockets. His arms and legs bowed outward like a chimpanzee's.

"Who I keep company with is my business," Drew said, heat rising to his ears. "Is that why you shot out my new windowpanes?"

"I never done it."

"The hell you didn't. Chantalene recognized your truck when you shot hers."

He sneered. "She's a lyin' bitch."

Drew hadn't hit a man since his sophomore year in college, and he didn't know he'd done it now until the pain knifed through his knuckles and up his right arm. Little Willie Bond sprawled backwards on the lawn. Drew heard Opal shriek, then slam the door and shoot the bolt.

"Get the gun, Ma!" Willie yelled from the ground, then scrambled to his feet. Drew spread his legs and braced himself, shifting away from the front window so he wouldn't get a shotgun blast in the back.

"Look, I didn't come here for a fight," he said, trying for a calm voice. "But you stay away from my house, and you stay away from Chantalene Morrell, or I'll have your ass in jail."

Small as Willie was, Drew fully expected him to launch an attack, and undoubtedly he would have if they hadn't been interrupted by the sound of another arrival.

The car parked next to Drew's and momentarily diverted Willie's attention. Martha Jenks stepped out of her dusty Buick and hailed them with a bright smile.

"Well, good morning, Drew! This is a surprise." She beamed at him, undoubtedly thinking he'd come on a neighborly social call.

"Morning, Martha." He hid his bloodied knuckles with his other hand but kept an eye on Little Willie while Martha approached.

Opal Bond opened the door again, her miniature handbag hanging over one arm. Mrs. Bond had been expecting Martha.

Martha looked from Drew's face to Opal's ashen one, to Little Willie, whose nose dripped blood, and her eyes changed but her smile never did. "Hello, Opal. I see you're ready."

Martha faced Willie, dwarfing him by two inches and thirty pounds. "I'm taking your mother over to El Rio to see Berta Jean today." Her voice was deliberate, patient, like a teacher instructing a stubborn child. "I'm sure you have no objection to that, do you, Willie?"

Little Willie's eyes narrowed with anger ... and something else. Fear? Clearly, he was intimidated by Martha's churchwoman sense of rightness. Drew watched him shrink another inch and begin to fidget under Martha's stern gaze. Her smile faded but never completely disappeared as she waited for him to answer. Opal hovered silently in the doorway.

"Berta Jean won't even know her," Willie said, grudgingly.

"Perhaps not," Martha said, "but we can never be sure what someone like Berta understands and what she doesn't. And I know your mother will feel better once she sees that Berta's being cared for properly." Her voice was kind, now; she had mothered the bully right out of Little Willie Bond. Drew fought back a smile.

Martha turned to Opal. "Shall we go?"

Opal squeezed out the door sideways, as if she'd be less visible that way, and passed in front of Willie without looking at him.

"How's the remodeling coming, Drew?" Martha asked pleasantly, as if she hadn't seen him only last night. She linked her arm through his and strolled him toward their cars. He knew he was being managed, but he didn't mind.

"Slowly," he said, and let her lead him away. "I still have windows to replace." He glared over his shoulder at Willie, who looked like a pressure cooker ready to blow off its safety valve.

Opal and Martha got into her car and Drew got in his. They drove off in tandem, with Drew imitating Martha's cheerful wave to Little Willie Bond.

In his rear view mirror, Drew saw Little Willie's return gesture, which was anything but cheerful.

# THIRTEEN

Standing in the early morning sunshine, Chantalene watched Drew's silver Volvo bump away from her house. *The smart-ass.*

Still, she smiled at the knowledge that he had wanted her this morning, despite the dangerous circumstances that put him on her couch overnight. Or maybe because of them. At any rate, his better judgment had overridden his impulses. Was he always ruled by common sense?

God, she hoped not.

She joined Bones on the front porch and gave her pal a morning head rub. "How did you like our houseguest, old girl? I notice you don't bark at him. Think we can trust him? Or were you just flirting?"

Bones' ecstatic expression had more to do with the massage than with any assessment of Drew Sander's character. "You're a pushover," Chantalene accused.

Before going inside, she glanced once more at the lingering trail of dust where Drew's car had disappeared.

In the kitchen, the aroma of French toast and scrambled eggs made her stomach growl. She felt ravenous. She filled her plate, doused the toast in maple syrup, and sat at the table with her plate and a cup of hot tea. She replayed the scene in the driveway in her mind, reflecting with some amazement that it was the first time in her life she had actually asked a man for a date. What a total social rookie.

What would she cook for Drew tomorrow night? Something hearty—the man ate like a lion. She ought to cook meat for him, but there was none in the house and Bond's Market was likely still closed. If it had re-opened, Little Willie probably would be minding the shop. When Big Willie was alive, Opal Bond wasn't allowed near the grocery, but Chantalene didn't want to chance running into Opal, either. What would she say? *Sorry your worthless husband is dead and can't beat you anymore?* Obviously, she couldn't go to the market.

She wondered if Opal's pathetic life would change for the better with her husband gone. More likely the woman would transfer her subservience to Little Willie, who was a replica of his father except in stature. Little Willie had learned to bully by his father's example.

She pulled out a yellow legal tablet from the pile of books and papers on the dining table. While she ate Drew's portion of eggs and toast, she sketched the four hooded figures from her dream, adding details from the waking memory that had returned to her in the El Rio jail. Flattening her pencil, she shaded the barn and pasture in the background. Then she marked the initials BWB where the face should be on one of the featureless forms. On another she lettered SJ, hesitated, and on a third, wrote LWB. These three she felt sure of. On the fourth figure that stood behind the others, she drew a question mark.

The maple syrup turned heavy and over-sweet in her mouth. She scraped the remainder of her breakfast into a bowl for Bones and rinsed her plate in the sink. Retrieving the drawing from the table, she took it to her bedroom and placed it out of sight in her roll-top desk. She slid the top shut and locked it, symbolically if not effectively putting the grisly memory out of her mind. Then she dressed in ragged black cutoffs and an old red t-shirt, her housecleaning clothes. She would make the house shine in honor of her first-ever dinner guest.

While she swept the braided rug with a broom, dust-mopped the corners, and scrubbed the bathroom fixtures until they shone, she hatched a plan.

She couldn't bear waiting around like a puddle duck for Little Willie to pot-shoot. Tonight she would stake out the Bond house, see where Little Willie went, what he did. If she was lucky, she might learn something she could present to Sheriff Justin as evidence—perhaps some clue about Big Willie's death. She knew it was far-fetched, maybe even risky, but she had to take some kind of action. She had to try to control her own fate.

With this decided, she began to relax. In the afternoon, she tied up her hair and weeded the garden, enjoying a mild sun that warmed her shoulders and deepened the tan on her bare legs. When her work was finished, she sat with Bones on the front porch, sharing a licorice stick.

Near sundown, she showered and changed into jeans, bridled Whippoorwill and stationed Bones to guard the house. By dusk she'd found an observation post on the service road to an oil well, a quarter mile from the Bond place.

Half the farms in Opalata County sported either an abandoned hole or a working oil well fitted with a pump and timer. This one was a working well, the access road freshly graveled. A sign beside it said "Katy #1," named for some farmer's wife or daughter. Mostly the wells were small producers with more gas than oil, a welcome supplement to an income hard-won from the soil. While the last red-orange streaks faded above the horizon, Chantalene dismounted behind a clump of trees that shielded her and Whip from view but allowed an unobstructed glimpse of Willie Bond's pickup parked in his yard.

Her eyes adjusted with the dark. Whippoorwill snuffled and nosed a clump of rye grass, complaining about the bit that hindered his chewing. "Sorry, fella. Can't help you right now," she said, patting his flank. She tried sitting on the ground but couldn't see the house and stood up again, leaning against the south side of a tree trunk stripped of branches by countless seasons of wind.

Lights glowed inside the Bond house and moonlight reflected off the truck. A granddaddy bullfrog cranked up his foghorn from a nearby pond, and somewhere a lonesome mourning dove cooed the blues. Once each hour, the pump on the oil well sprang to life, shaking her heart in her chest. Other than that, absolutely nothing happened. Her head grew heavy and she rested it against the tree.

She'd begun to nod when a car door slammed, jerking her alert. Headlights flashed on in the Bond's driveway. It was midnight, and Little Willie was on the move.

His pickup pulled out of the driveway and turned east.

She mounted Whippoorwill and followed at a trot, her heart racing faster than Whip's hoofbeats. Luckily, Little Willie drove as if he had all the time in the world to get where he was going. The land here was flat and it was easy to keep the pickup's taillights in sight.

Willie passed the road that would have led him to town—or to her house—and headed out of the flat farmland into the wooded foothills of the Black Forks. She urged Whip into a lope lest Little Willie leave them too far behind. Moonlight made it easy to see the road. No other cars were about.

They'd gone several miles and Whip was tiring when, far ahead of her, Willie pulled off the road and doused his lights.

Chantalene slowed Whip to a walk. Willie's interior light popped on and then off. She made out his shape as he walked toward another vehicle, a dark-colored van parked in the entrance to a pasture. Willie got into the van, riding shotgun, and she heard the engine start. The van moved forward into the field and disappeared behind a line of trees.

Accomplices. Her stomach fluttered. Playing private detective suddenly seemed pretty stupid. She had no idea how many people might be inside the van, or whether they were armed. One thing was certain, though; if they'd wanted to be observed, they wouldn't be out here in the dead of night. If they saw her and gave chase, no way could she and Whip escape.

She wished for Sheriff Justin, or Drew, or a cell phone. And knew that if she could contact either of them, they'd tell her to go home and leave the cloak-and-dagger stuff to the law.

But what was Little Willie doing out here? If she could find out without being seen, she'd be delighted to let the sheriff take it from there.

She walked the horse closer and dismounted in the shadows of a hedgerow, tying Whip's bridle to a branch. Her tennis shoes sinking into the soft earth, she angled across a plowed field toward the place where the van had disappeared.

A well-worn tire track marked the spot. She followed it, staying underneath the trees along the fence line when she could. Damp fallen leaves cushioned the sound of her steps. Every few seconds she stopped to listen: tree frogs and the distant hoot of an owl, but no car engine. The wind was uncommonly still.

It was hard to tell how far she'd gone through unfamiliar land in the dark. She guessed she'd been walking twenty minutes when a distinct chopping sound rose from the brush ahead, thickening her throat. She froze, squatting low to the ground, and heard an ominous rustling of bushes.

But the rustle wasn't getting closer, and now she heard voices, one of them Willie's, giving orders. The two that answered sounded like teenagers. Using their noise for cover, she crept closer. Carefully, soundlessly, she climbed a mulberry tree that still held enough leaves to keep her hidden.

From her perch she looked across a tangle of short brush and onto a patch of tall, lush plants.

Marijuana. Little Willie and his boys were harvesting.

She straddled a limb of the tree and watched them stack fronds into the back of the van. They worked at a relaxed pace, apparently unworried about detection, talking and laughing in the shadows of the tall plants. Every few minutes one or the other stopped to pop open a beer or take a whiz in the bushes.

Chantalene sat motionless, trying to connect the scene before her with shattered windows and a corpulent corpse, while the night around her cooled toward morning. None of it made sense.

The two Willies must have been trafficking in dope for years. That might explain Opal Bond's new house, but could it have something to do with the senior Bond's murder? Actually, she doubted it. This wasn't exactly drug-lord country. People had been growing maryjane in these hills since she was in school, but there were plenty of markets for everybody's crop with no concerns over competition. Except for an occasional raid by the Oklahoma State Bureau of Investigation, nobody paid much attention.

Her discovery might get Little Willie temporarily arrested, a thought that gave her a certain satisfaction. But it seemed a separate issue from Big Willie's murder, unless greed over the profits had driven a wedge between father and son.

Most certainly, it proved nothing about the lynching of Clyde Morrell.

Her leg cramped and she needed to pee. She wanted out of that tree, but getting down posed more of a noise problem than getting up, and the boys chose that moment to take a break from their labors. They sat cross-legged on the ground beside the van and began passing around a sample of their refined product. She dared not move.

She could see the glow of the reefer as each one took a hit. This could be a favorable development. Sure enough, in a few minutes they began to talk funny and laugh at nothing in particular. Even when she fell the last four feet descending from the tree, Little Willie and the boys never noticed. So much for the theory that grass heightens sensory perceptions.

She retraced her path along the tree line, casting frequent glances over her shoulder while she squatted behind a bush. At the edge of the pasture she surprised a coyote hunting for field mice, or rather it surprised her. Catching her scent, the animal dropped its head and leapt into the trees, but its sudden appearance chilled her bones.

The eastern sky lightened and turned magenta while she jogged across the plowed field toward the clump of trees where Whip waited. The earth smelled fresh and the dawn might have been inspiring, but she was too tired to care.

They headed home at a walk, stopping by a stock tank to let Whippoorwill drink. She judged it close to eight before they meandered up the driveway to her house.

Drew Sander's car was parked in front.

She smiled and felt her heart beat speed up a notch. But her smile faded when she considered the hour. An unlikely time of day for a visit.

She clucked to Whip and urged him forward, but

the exhausted horse refused to increase his pace. They approached the house at a walk.

Drew wasn't in his car, or anywhere to be seen. Maybe he'd gone inside to wait for her. Had she forgotten to lock the door? Bones stood on the front porch, wagging her tail, and Chantalene scowled at her gullible watchdog.

Dropping Whip's reins beside the porch railing, she dismounted and climbed the steps without sound. The front door stood slightly open, and she peered through the screen.

He wasn't in the living room. She pushed the door open slowly and stepped into the eerie silence, her neck hair crawling with a sudden vision of Drew's limp body sprawled in some corner of the house ...

She stepped quietly. He wasn't in the kitchen.

Nothing seemed disturbed. With a sense of foreboding she moved silently down the hall. The bathroom door was open; no one inside. She came to her bedroom doorway and stopped.

Drew sat at her small black desk in the corner of the bedroom, his back toward her. He was quite alive, and *he was going through her things.*

Anger tightened her chest until she could barely breathe. She saw her baby book placed to one side, and her only snapshot of her parents. The one doll she'd ever owned, blue eyes open in its china face, the red dress streaked and faded. Her most personal things! *What the hell did he think he was doing?*

Her fists clenched. She wanted to scream but her voice froze in her throat. For a moment she was a stranger, seeing the room with other eyes. The worn area rug, the black-painted furniture, the white comforter on her bed strewn with pillows ... the closet door standing open, her clothes hanging gaunt and aligned like a stranger's, or like her mother's—all red and black. She didn't own a shirt or a pair of jeans in any other colors. How strange it would seem, to anyone who didn't know LaVita.

The books in her shelves, too—*A History of Gypsies in Europe, Spells and Incantations, Case Studies in Extra-Sensory Perception.* Without knowing her mother, or how hard Chantalene had tried to preserve her memory, her life must appear peculiar indeed.

*And it was none of his fucking business.*

At last she found her voice. "What the hell are you doing?"

Drew jumped, tearing one corner from the paper he was holding. The paper fluttered to the floor—her drawing of four hooded phantoms from her dream.

The roll-top desk had been locked; she was certain of that. The key had been in her lingerie drawer.

Caught, he took the offensive. "You lied to me."

*"Get out of my things."*

She delivered each word like a separate bullet, standing in the doorway with her face on fire.

"You do know who they are, don't you?" he said. "You labeled Big Willie and SJ ... Slim Jenks." His voice sounded thick and weird.

*"Get out of my house."*

Her eyes went to the snapshot on the desktop, the image of a dark-haired couple she'd burned into her mind so she wouldn't forget what they looked like. Clyde's arm held LaVita close against his side as they smiled into the camera, her red-and-black flowered skirt blowing around her knees.

A flicker of regret crossed Drew's face. For a moment he was the friend who'd stayed the night on her couch, the man she'd almost invited into her bed. "I'm sorry for invading your privacy," he said. "But I have to know where you've been all night."

"I don't have to tell you where I've been, tonight or ever!"

The hard look returned to his eyes. He doesn't trust me, she thought.

"I've just come from Slim Jenks' place," he said and paused, watching her face as if for a reaction. "He's dead."

Her eyes blinked once. "Dead?"

"Monkey found him early this morning, when he went out to check on him and take the food Martha sent."

"Murdered?"

"They're saying suicide." A muscle in his jaw twitched. "It's hard to do with a shotgun, but not impossible."

She closed her eyes a moment, remembering the old bachelor's hollow face. Damn. Though she couldn't forgive Slim Jenks for his role in her father's death, she hadn't wished him dead.

She blinked again, and her anger returned. "What's that got to do with your snooping through my house?"

"They found a hand-written will. Slim left everything to Monkey except his collector violin." He watched her face, frowning.

"So?"

"He left the violin to you."

Her mouth opened, then closed. She shook her head slowly.

Drew's elbow bumped the doll. The eyes rolled shut and it cried like a cat, eerie and plaintive in the stillness. He cringed.

"Why would Slim leave you something so valuable?"

"Atonement."

"It implicates you in his death."

"That's absurd!"

"Chantalene, *where have you been?*"

She strode to the desk and slammed the cover in one

fluid motion, barely missing his fingers. "Get the hell out of my house!"

He stood and faced her, not budging. "Someone's killing off the hangmen, aren't they?" He watched her face. "For all I know, it could be you."

She threw up her hands. "If that's what you think, you can go to hell." She whirled and started for the door.

He caught her arm. "Hold it a minute! I'm listed as your attorney of record. I think you owe me some answers."

She twisted free. "I don't owe you anything! If you think I'm a murderer, take your damned name off my case and stay away from me. Nothing gives you the right to paw through ... "

Her eyes flickered to the desk again, where her memories lay exposed, and her vision blurred. She bolted from the room.

By the time he followed, she was out the front door and astride Whippoorwill, gouging the surprised gelding with her heels. Whip lurched into action.

"Chantalene, wait!"

His shout sounded both angry and pleading. She heard him kick the porch post and swear.

She galloped Whippoorwill across the field, his hooves pounding the wilted vegetables. The wind whipped her hair and the familiar anger surged inside her ribcage. In her ears she heard the echo of her mother's horrible scream ... a scream of helplessness and anger.

Behind her, Drew's car engine caught and roared, coming after her. She headed for the fence line.

Two gnarled strands of barbwire separated her property from the pasture behind Animal Draw, where the hay barn stood. She crouched forward on the horse and dug in her knees. Whippoorwill lifted as if in slow motion and cleared the low fence, landing heavily but keeping his feet. Her body slammed against the horse's back and she heard car tires skid in the dust behind her. Whip raced on across the pasture.

She never saw what made the horse stumble, but she felt his front leg crumple and go down.

And then she was flying; soaring in a slow, flat arc over the horse's head. She hit the pasture full face and her body twisted, her weight coming down hard on her left leg. For an instant, everything was quiet. She felt no pain.

Whippoorwill whinnied. She heard Drew yell, running toward her. He dropped to his knees in the grass. "Don't move."

Her face felt serrated and now a nauseating pain rose upward from her left leg. She spit grass. Touching her fingers to her upper lip, she found blood leaking from her nose.

She closed her eyes and felt herself falling.

Whippoorwill gave another distressed whinny and Chantalene struggled to sit up but couldn't. She held herself on one elbow, wincing. "Check on Whip. He's hurt," she said.

Gently, Drew touched her knee. "Can you move your leg?"

"Ow! Maybe in a minute. *Please* check on Whip!"

Drew went to the horse, which lay upright only a few paces away. He examined the horse's leg and freed the hoof from a piece of splintered wood. Several paces behind him she could see a black hole in the grass.

"What is it?" she called.

"There used to be a farmhouse here, long before my time," Drew said. "I'd forgotten about it. Whippoorwill's foot went through the rotted cover of an old storm cellar that was grown over with grass. Apparently the cellar was never filled in."

A sinking feeling melted through her chest. "Is his leg broken?"

Drew hesitated. "I'm pretty sure."

"Shit. Poor Whip." She slumped back in the grass.

Drew patted Whip's neck and spoke soothingly, and the horse relaxed onto his side. His round belly heaved and he shuddered. Tears mixed with the blood on Chantalene's face.

Drew came back and leaned over her, checking for other injuries. She saw his jaw tighten.

"I suspect you've broken something, as well."

She grasped the front of his shirt. "Listen to me. Don't let them shoot him! Get the vet from El Rio. They can set horses' legs just like people's, and *I will not have them shoot my horse.* Do you hear me?"

"Nobody will shoot him," he promised. "Or you either." He brushed the hair from her forehead and smiled, but his face looked pinched and serious.

He stood and looked back across the field toward his distant car and her house beyond, considering. Then he glanced back at the shattered cellar door, saw something, and frowned.

"What? What is it?" she asked.

"Something white. Like bone ... "

At first she thought he meant Whip's leg was shattered, the bone protruding. But instead he knelt and tore a rotted board away from the gaping hole in the lid of the old storm cellar, and then another. A musty, rancid odor floated to her. She struggled to sit up, feeling a sick, nameless dread.

"What is it?" she demanded. She tried to drag herself toward him.

"Don't! Don't come over here."

The pain stopped her and she lay back, panting. Her head pounded.

Drew crouched beside the exposed cavern, holding his breath, and leaned over to peer inside. Then he turned his head away and swallowed hard, his face white.

"Oh God, Chantalene."

The tone of his voice struck her chest like stone, eclipsing the pain in her leg.

"I'm so sorry," he said. "I think we've found your mother."

# FOURTEEN

Chantalene lay on her back in the pasture, her left leg throbbing. She squeezed her eyes shut and fought to hold onto the image of her mother alive, vibrant, and smiling. But it wasn't enough to overpower the knowledge of what lay at the bottom of the storm cellar a few feet away—a human skeleton shrouded in black and red cloth.

Drew knelt beside the ragged opening to the cave, his head hung low. For once he was speechless.

*All this time, she was here,* Chantalene thought, *while I lived my life, oblivious to her disintegration over the years.*

Every breath sent a streak of pain through her hip. Even worse was the heartache of knowing at long last why LaVita never came back for her. Drew came to her and sat in the grass. She couldn't look at him. "I'll run to the house and phone for help," he said finally. "I'll be back as fast as I can. Don't try to move, promise?"

She nodded, her eyes still closed. She listened as his footsteps retreated, running, then surrendered the tears she been saving a decade for her mother. Her beautiful, black-haired Gypsy mother ... how had she come to rest in this godforsaken place? Who had done this to her?

*The truck careened into the Jenkses' driveway and skidded to a halt. Dust rose from beneath the tires as LaVita jumped out of the cab and pulled her across the seat. A thousand questions she dared not ask dissolved like the dust in her mouth.*

*LaVita dragged her, stumbling, up the walkway to the front door. Her mother's fierce grip stung her arm. In her trailing hand Chantalene clutched a pillowcase containing a change of clothes, her hairbrush, the china-faced doll; and in her mind she carried the image of the shed collapsing in flames.*

*The house was dark. LaVita pounded on the door, pounded again, the awful whining hum rising in her throat again as she stamped from one foot to the other, calling Martha's name. LaVita's shoulders shook and her eyes glittered in the darkness like some wild animal.*

*"Mama?" The grip on her arm tightened in answer and LaVita pounded on the door again.*

*A light came on inside; the curtain moved. The door opened and Martha Jenks appeared wearing a flannel nightgown. Her long braid hung across her shoulder as she leaned to open the screen door. She looked wide-awake.*

*"LaVita! In the name of heaven! What's wrong?"*

*"They're going to kill me! Please keep Chantalene with you!"*

*"What on earth ... Who's going to kill you? Come inside!"*

*"No time! I have to get away! Please keep my baby safe."*

*"No, Mama! Don't leave me!"*

*LaVita's voice broke. "Please ... if they find me ... "*

*"Of course she can stay, but ... "*

*Headlights flashed across the driveway, turning in. A wail like a bugle rose from LaVita's throat. She grabbed her daughter by the shoulders and looked for one instant into her eyes.*

*"Mama, no!"*

*LaVita hugged her fiercely, whispering in her ear. "I'll come back for you. Don't ever tell what you saw!"*

*And she was off the porch and into the idling truck, jamming it in gear as Martha stepped onto the porch and shouted. "It's only Monkey coming back from El Rio! Wait! LaVita! It's just Monkey!"*

*But LaVita was gone.*

The vibrations of Drew's footsteps pounded across the pasture, returning. Chantalene thought irrationally of the Indians who'd once listened to this ground for the hooves of buffalo. All those lives, gone forever. She felt as ancient as the land. And realized she was going into shock.

She forced one deep breath after another. Tears stung the crosshatched scratches on her face and she blotted her eyes on the sleeve of her shirt.

Bones had followed Drew from the house. Spotting her in the grass, the dog bounded ahead. Chantalene braced her arms to ward Bones away from her leg, leaving her face vulnerable to wet doggy kisses. Oh well. She'd read somewhere that dog saliva had healing properties.

Drew knelt beside her, out of breath, frowning. "How are you doing?"

"All right."

He slipped his wadded jacket beneath her head. "I called the vet, too, and she's on her way. I had to cut your fence so the ambulance can drive down here."

"I think I could get to the house if you'd—"

"Absolutely not. If that thighbone is fractured, we could do a lot of damage moving you. Just stay put and let somebody else take care of things, for a change." He brushed grass from her hair and sat beside her, holding her hand.

They waited. "For both our sakes, I hope it's too late in the year for chiggers," he said.

She tried to smile but felt too sleepy, too defeated to open her eyes. Her tongue felt thick and dry.

Inside the peach-red world behind her eyelids, fatigue rolled over her, washing up the image of her mother's face again, tight and terrified the last time Chantalene had seen her. Tears seeped between her eyelashes. She'd known all these years that LaVita must be dead, yet the pain in her chest was as fresh as if she were twelve years old again, abandoned for reasons she couldn't understand.

The drone of a car coming across the pasture roused her and she opened her eyes. The vet had arrived before the ambulance, which said a lot about life in Tetumka. Chantalene was glad, though. She couldn't have let them haul her away with poor Whippoorwill still lying there.

Dr. Linda Majors was a good vet. She checked Whip thoroughly and set his leg, with help from a very white-faced tax attorney. By the time the ambulance did arrive, Linda had Whippoorwill up on three legs and was leading him slowly back to the corral, with Bones following.

Sheriff Justin had arrived, too, to recover the remains from the cellar. The sheriff stood over her a moment, holding his hat in both hands, his silhouette large against the sky. "I'm really sorry about your mother, Chantalene," he said.

The sheriff and his deputy stalled around, obviously waiting until she was loaded into the ambulance so she wouldn't have to see them remove her mother's bones. Feeling nauseated, she laid her head back on the stretcher and wished for sleep, wished she never had to wake up again.

But she did awaken, in the El Rio Hospital emergency room. The staff surprised her with their efficiency, in spite of her lack of insurance. The x-ray showed a cracked tibia in her left lower leg. Which seemed odd, since it was her hip that hurt the most.

Drew walked beside her to surgery, where they would set the bone. And he was there when she awoke in a private room with a cast that ran from the top of her left thigh to her toes. Her sprained wrist had rated a splint and elastic bandage. Drew sat in a chair beside the bed holding her other hand. She'd barely awakened enough to smile at him when a nurse came in, checked her vitals, and injected her with something that made her feel thick and fuzzy, and soon she felt nothing at all.

When she awoke again, it was night. Drew was slumped in the chair beside the bed, his head slung back, mouth open. The sight of him still there made her nose burn, her anger at his snooping washed away by his flood of attention. After the argument they had, he might have gone home and left her, but he didn't. That said something about his character, and it was something she admired. Besides, how could she blame him for being suspicious of her after Slim's death? In his shoes, she'd have been suspicious, too.

A pattern of light played across the ceiling from the half-open door. She listened to the lonely night sounds of the hospital and thought about her mother.

What was the last thing LaVita had seen before she died? Did she draw her last breaths in that cellar among the spiders and the dark? Injured, unable to climb the steps? Did she think of the daughter she was leaving behind?

Would an autopsy show how she died?

The ache in Chantalene's chest made it hard to breathe. She pulled her mind away from thoughts of how her mother died and tried to think of the days ahead. She ought to plan a funeral of some sort. Bury LaVita's remains in the cemetery next to her father's.

How would she pay for it? Or this hospital room?

She thought of Whippoorwill standing in his pen with his broken leg, and of Slim Jenks putting the business end of a shotgun in his mouth and staring down the barrel while he reached out a long arm to pull the trigger.

Maybe Slim's answer wasn't such a bad one. He must have felt his guilt like the pain she felt now from grief. Day after day, unrelenting. And her visit to him that night had probably amplified it beyond endurance.

She might not have chosen a shotgun for the method, but she could sympathize with its results.

A nurse came in on quiet feet and offered her a pill. She swallowed it without even caring what it was.

When she woke again it was morning. Her leg throbbed and she needed to pee. Drew was still breathing heavily, slumped in the chair. Poor guy. How could he sleep bent sideways like that? She pushed the call button pinned to her pillow.

A plump nurse of indeterminate age whisked in, efficiency etched into her plain features. Chantalene whispered, "Can you help me to the bathroom?"

"You're not to put any weight on your leg today," the nurse said, her voice loud in the quiet room. "You'll have to use this." She held up a contorted plastic bottle.

Chantalene groaned. If she had four legs like Whippoorwill, she wouldn't have to suffer such indignity.

Drew awoke, his hair standing up on one side of his head and his eyes unfocused. When he saw the urinal, he bolted from the chair. "I'll be back in a few minutes," he mumbled, and fled.

The nurse, whose name was Jan, helped Chantalene use the bottle, then cleaned her up and brushed her hair. She was just leaving when Drew came back carrying a Styrofoam silo of coffee for him and a cup of hot tea for her.

None too soon, either, because the caffeine helped

fortify her for the parade of visitors that followed. She had no idea she was so popular.

Dr. Phelps, who'd set her leg, came first. He checked her cast and assorted bruises. The doctor was sixtyish, with wire-rimmed glasses and a pink, balding head, and he smiled a lot.

"You can go home tomorrow if you have someone to stay with you," he said. "I want you to keep the weight off this leg a few days."

Drew volunteered. She wasn't sure how they'd work out the bathroom thing, but she was feeling a bit shaky emotionally as well as physically, and the idea of not going home alone sounded fine.

Luckily, the cast would prevent her from jumping Drew's bones.

After breakfast—cream of wheat with cinnamon toast, which she was grateful Drew declined to share—Sheriff Justin came in. He placed a brown paper bag on the floor beside the footstool where he sat down.

"I'd ask how you're feeling, but it has to be rotten," he said. He didn't sound as if he felt much better. "You going to be okay?"

His gray eyes assessed her. The stubble of his beard looked grayer today, and deep creases made parentheses around his mouth. Chantalene knew he had his calloused hands full. First Willie Bond's murder, then Slim Jenks' suicide, and now the discovery of the bones in the cellar, all of them falling under his jurisdiction. She almost felt sorry for him.

"I believe I was supposed to check in with you," she said, "so here I am."

He turned his hat around and around in his hands. "I'm real sorry about your mother," he said, for the second time.

Her stomach rolled. “There’s no doubt, then? The bones are hers?” The fatigue and black dread rose up again. Her arms felt weak and she laid her head back against the pillow.

The sheriff cleared his throat, looked down at the toes of his scuffed boots. “Actually, for the record, I need a positive identification from the next of kin.” He picked up the paper sack. “I hate to ask you this, Chantalene.”

He pulled a clear plastic bag from the sack and looked up at her, as if for permission. She nodded and swallowed the lump in her throat. Sheriff Justin handed her the plastic bag. Sealed inside were remnants of black fabric printed with red roses.

Her mother’s skirt. The same one she’d worn in the snapshot that lay on her desk at home. She looked away.

Drew sat with his eyes on the floor, elbows braced on his spread knees.

Chantalene lifted the bag again and traced the outline of a rose with her finger. She had to clear her throat before she could speak. “Yes, it’s my mother’s,” she said finally. “What did you do with ... her remains?”

Sheriff Justin replaced the bag in his brown paper sack. “They’re being analyzed. We should have a report this afternoon.”

“Will it show cause of death?”

“I don’t know. She’d been there a long time.”

“Probably twelve years,” Chantalene said. She closed her eyes and laid her head back on the pillow.

In the long silence that followed, she thought, *I’ll move away from this cursed county, to a big, anonymous city. Get a regular job. Maybe take a new name.*

“We brought in Little Willie Bond on that matter of shooting out windows,” the sheriff said. He glanced at Drew, who still stared at the floor. “He’s gonna be with us a couple days, at least.”

"I found his marijuana field," she said. "He and his buddies were harvesting last night. No, I guess it was the night before." She was too tired to keep it straight.

The sheriff's eyebrows rose. "Really? That could help us take Little Willie out of circulation for quite a while."

She described the location of the field and the two teenagers she'd seen helping Willie.

"That's where you were the night Slim Jenks died? Tailing Little Willie around the county?"

Now Drew looked up.

"That's where I was," she said tiredly. "All by myself."

"And you wonder why I kept you in protective custody?" The sheriff twirled his hat, shaking his head. "Doc says there's no reason to doubt Slim's suicide. But Chantalene, why would he leave you that valuable fiddle?"

She closed her eyes. "Because somebody talked him into helping hang my father, and he regretted it every day since."

Sheriff Justin bowed his head, said nothing, and quietly left. Chantalene closed her eyes and let depression engulf her. Drew came to the bed, squeezed her hand, and didn't let go.

"I'm glad you're here," she said. She saw the knot of his Adam's apple move up and down his throat, and his blue eyes filled.

Later that morning, Thelma Patterson stuck her head in the door. "Everybody decent?" she sang out. As if that would stop her from coming in.

"Come on in, Thelma," Chantalene said and smiled at Drew. Comic relief.

Thelma set a fruit jar of blue asters on the table beside the bed. A sweet, floral scent wafted over her, either the flowers or Thelma's perfume. Drew stood up and offered Thelma his chair.

"Aren't you supposed to be at the post office?" Chantalene asked.

"It's Sunday, silly! Don't they allow you a calendar in here?"

Chantalene smiled. "I'd sort of lost track."

Thelma plopped into the chair and patted Chantalene's unbandaged arm. "Want me to hold your mail for a couple days? Be glad to bring it to you later."

"I appreciate that, Thelma, but I'm going home tomorrow."

"Good for you, honey! A hospital's no place for sick people, I always say. They never let you get any sleep." She looked approvingly from Chantalene to Drew and back again. "Lucky you have a close neighbor to look in on you."

When neither of them took the bait, Thelma leaned toward the bed, sympathy softening her plump face. "I'm so sorry about your mother. Have they found out the cause of death yet?"

"No, but it wasn't any accident."

"I suppose not. How awful." Thelma shook her head, her eyes intense. "How did you manage to find her?"

"Actually, Whippoorwill found her, and broke his leg in the process."

Thelma tisked. "So I heard."

Chantalene was certain Thelma knew every detail of her accident by now, except maybe what Drew was doing out there in the pasture with her. She'd leave that to the postmistress' imagination.

"At least you finally know what happened to her," Thelma said. "That's more than I ever knew about my husband, Billy Ray."

Chantalene could picture Billy Ray running—as far

from the throes of Tetumka gossip as he could get—but she didn't say so.

Thelma chattered a few minutes about other peoples' business, then turned her attention to Drew, who was leaning quietly in the corner.

"How's the divorce coming?" she asked brightly. "I noticed you got papers from a law firm the other day."

Drew looked so flustered that Chantalene almost laughed.

"Umm, fine. It's going fine," he stammered.

His response bored Thelma enough to conclude her visit. After she left, Chantalene sent Drew home, too.

"You look exhausted. Go get some rest. And would you please stop by and check on Whippoorwill? And put out dog food for Bones?"

"No problem," he said predictably. Someday she'd cure him of that phrase, she decided. But not today.

He stood beside the bed, hesitant about leaving. "What if you need something and can't get a nurse? They're always short-handed on Sundays."

"Then I'll yell until they pay attention," she said. "Actually, I'll probably just sleep."

"I'll be back tomorrow morning to take you home," he said.

She nodded and tried to smile, missing him already. He lifted her unbandaged hand and kissed her fingers, a gesture so tender it almost stopped her heart.

When he'd gone, the room felt empty.

At lunch, she ate the salad on her tray but didn't touch the odoriferous Swiss steak. The nurse took the tray away, and Chantalene was on the verge of dozing when Martha and Monkey Jenks came in, still in their church clothes.

Monkey looked sad and strained. Even Martha, who never displayed a ruffled feather, showed webs of worry lines at the corners of her eyes. With all they had to worry about, Chantalene felt touched that they'd come to see her.

Martha leaned over the bed, smelling like talcum powder. "I'm so sorry about LaVita."

How long would it take before she could think of her mother without the lump rising to her throat? "Thanks. And I'm sorry about Slim."

Someone had once told her—probably Thelma—that Slim had been sweet on Martha in high school, but she'd married Monkey instead. A better choice for a husband, no doubt.

"It was an awful shock. Monkey's been really upset," Martha said, as if he weren't standing right there beside the bed, hat in hand. Monkey looked old today, and ill at ease. Chantalene knew he hated hospitals.

"How you doing, little lady?" he said.

"Pretty good, considering. We're supposed to get the medical examiner's report on my mother this afternoon," she said, then regretted it, realizing that Monkey might be waiting on autopsy results, as well.

Martha came to the rescue, changing the subject. "How long are they going to keep you here?"

"Just until tomorrow. Drew volunteered to nurse-maid for me, so the doc would turn me loose."

Martha's face looked injured. "I could stay with you," she said. "Wouldn't you rather have a woman?"

"At certain times, undoubtedly. But you have your hands full right now. Please don't worry about me." Wasted words.

"Nonsense. I'll take turns with Drew, at least. Best cure for sorrow is to help somebody else."

Chantalene sighed. If anyone was in need, it was always Martha on the spot. Only an ungrateful scum would resent her eternal good deeds. *I am scum.*

With nothing else to talk about, the Jenkses wished her well and went home. Alone in the quiet room, Chantalene lay frowning. In their wake, she was aware of a niggling, insistent impression that she couldn't quite isolate.

Something was wrong with Monkey.

Never talkative, he was obviously grieving for Slim, as well. But no rational explanation quite dispelled the peculiar aura of ... *distress? fear?* ... that had hovered around him today. Though he and Martha hadn't said a word to each other while they were there, Chantalene sensed tension between them.

The more she tried to account for the feeling, the more unsettling it felt.

# FIFTEEN

Outside the hospital, Drew stood bareheaded in the rain waiting for a nurse to wheel Chantalene down the incline to his waiting car. It was another mark of the past on him that he enjoyed the rain, he thought, especially the way it smelled. Farmers always liked rain, except at harvest time. Now harvest was long over, and so was the summer heat.

Chantalene held a large black umbrella high enough to shelter both her and the nurse who leaned over the wheelchair. Chantalene's mouth formed a hard line of impatience. She had put up a fuss about riding in the chair instead of walking. In all his days, he'd never met anyone so stubborn.

The three of them managed to angle Chantalene's leg cast crosswise in the front floorboard. Drew had pushed the front seat of the Volvo all the way back, but it was still a tight fit. For the second time in two days, he wished for a nice, roomy pickup.

He tossed a set of crutches into the back seat. Dr. Phelps had given her a strict admonition not to use them for a couple of days, until the swelling and soreness subsided. Drew could see it would be up to him to enforce the edict. He handed her Thelma's jar of asters, waved to Nurse Jan, and went around to climb behind the wheel.

"How about some non-institutional lunch?" he asked.

"Surely there's a café in town that serves veggie burgers. We could eat in the car."

Chantalene laid her head back against the seat. Her face looked pale and he suspected the leg was hurting, though she wouldn't tell him. "I'm not hungry," she said. "But get yourself something, if you like."

He drove on. Missing lunch wouldn't kill him.

At the edge of town they passed the Piggly Wiggly. He thought about stopping for groceries but didn't want to leave her in the car alone. He hoped she had something in her refrigerator besides alfalfa sprouts and tofu.

She was uncharacteristically quiet on the ride home. Her eyes seemed to slip over the small houses outside the car window without really seeing them. After a couple of attempts at aimless conversation, he gave in to the silence.

Each day since they'd found her mother's bones, she seemed more depressed. He was less worried about her physical injuries than this listless, brown mood. He didn't know whether he should try to cheer her up, or just leave her alone.

Within a few miles the drizzle lightened and then stopped. He turned off the wipers and thought about the odd circumstances that had cast him as caregiver—one of several unaccustomed roles he'd assumed in the week he'd been back in Oklahoma.

The rain had missed Tetumka, and Chantalene's driveway was only muddy in the ruts. Approaching the house, they could see Whippoorwill standing forlornly in the corral, favoring his bandaged leg.

"Poor Whip," she said.

"You two can sign each other's casts," he offered. But she didn't laugh.

The house, too, looked sad with its patch of plywood tacked

over the broken front window. He'd have to get that fixed. The flowers in her window boxes had wilted and he promised to water them. They parked close to the front porch.

Thank goodness for Bones. The high-energy shepherd bounded to the car, wagging all over. It was the first time in days Drew had seen Chantalene smile. When she opened the door, the dog tried to jump into her lap, spilling water from the jar of flowers.

"I missed you, too," she said, wrapping Bones in a one-armed hug.

He carried her inside, angling her stiff leg through the doorway. The cast felt heavier than her body. As they maneuvered down the short hall to her bedroom, he suffered a flashback of contrition for their last encounter there. If he hadn't trespassed, she wouldn't have broken her leg. Nor discovered LaVita's fate. She'd wanted the truth about her mother, but maybe she'd have been better off without it.

He settled her beneath the comforter, set a glass of water within reach, then stood beside the bed feeling an awkward lack of anything to do.

"How about a game of gin rummy?"

"You don't have to entertain me. I think I might sleep a while."

He nodded. "That would be good." He hesitated again, then opened his empty hands. "I'll be in the living room. If you need anything, yell."

He retrieved the crutches and his duffle from the car. The bag contained only toiletries and a change of clothes, not enough to bother unpacking. Feeling useless, he sat on the sofa and looked around, wishing for a TV. Then he wished for a cigarette—the first time in two days he'd even thought about smoking. Nothing like calamity to help you break old habits.

Pacing, he scanned the bookshelf but felt too restless to read. He looked over Chantalene's computer, which she'd told him she bought second-hand during her first semester in college. The machine was an outmoded version of the same kind he used in his office in New York—and that reminded him of the letters from Emily and her lawyer, now stuffed in the glove compartment of his car. He went out and got them.

"Mind if I use your computer?" he called toward the bedroom.

"Help yourself," came the drowsy answer.

He reread the lawyer's letter first, the less painful of the two. It was a settlement agreement, neatly typed up for his signature. Sign here, Mr. Sander, and give away your furniture, your wife, and $2,000 a month rent for the apartment where she'll continue to live as long as she chooses.

Right.

He opened Emily's letter.

"Dear Drew." A nice, friendly start. "My attorney has drawn up a settlement offer and you should get it in the mail soon. I hope you'll consider signing it quickly and getting this unhappy business over with. I don't expect any alimony ... " what did she call $2,000 a month rent? " ... but I'd like to keep the furniture, since I picked it out and I plan to stay in the apartment."

*And where should I stay? At the YMCA? No need for furniture there.*

She closed with a pointed reference to his neglected job in her father's firm, and an offhand wish for his good health.

No shit. If he didn't stay healthy, he might not be able to pay her rent.

Ah, Emily the Emasculator. It was somehow comforting to know she hadn't changed, and that the divorce wasn't a mistake. He laid both letters beside the computer and switched it on. While Chantalene slept, he would draft a counter offer to Emily's proposed settlement.

He started typing. Emily could keep the apartment and the furniture, except for his grandmother's rocking chair. No problem there; Emily had always hated that chair. He also bequeathed her their joint membership in the trendy health club where they'd never once gone together to work out. He didn't really care about those things. He agreed to pay *half* her rent for six months, long enough for her to settle unexpected expenses and adjust to living on her own income. They hadn't accumulated joint savings, but they each had mutual funds and neither of them would be financially embarrassed.

In his view, the document was more than fair. Emily was a talented interior designer, quite capable of making as much money as he did. She worked on commission, though, and now she'd have to hustle to keep up her accustomed standard of living. Of course, if she got into debt, her daddy would bail her out.

After two false starts, he figured out the print commands on the computer and his masterpiece of civil legalese droned off Chantalene's antiquated, dot-matrix machine. The document didn't look like Wm. Bratten, Esq.'s work, but it sounded lawyerly and confident. He looked it over and smiled.

*The man who has himself for an attorney has a fool for a client.* What the hell.

The phone shrilled, springing him from his chair like a startled frog. He ran to the kitchen to snatch the receiver before the noise woke Chantalene.

"How are you two doing over there?" Martha Jenks' voice sounded strained, compared to her usual heartiness.

"Okay, I guess. Chantalene's asleep." He knew Chantalene

sometimes resented Martha's motherly concern, but he was grateful to Martha for checking on them. "She's really depressed," he confided, "and I don't know what to say to make her feel better."

"It'll just take time, I imagine. Do you need anything?" she asked. "I could bring you a casserole. So many folks have sent food over here my kitchen looks like a delicatessen. Monkey and I can never use it all."

He'd forgotten the country custom of bringing food to a house struck by tragedy. His lunchless stomach growled, and he fantasized a huge baking dish full of meat and cheese and potatoes. But Martha had problems of her own.

"We're fine," he said. "I imagine you've had a pretty lousy day."

"The funeral's tomorrow morning." She puffed a sigh. "I'll be glad when it's over. Don't you worry about attending," she added quickly. "Chantalene shouldn't be left alone. Monkey will understand."

Then her voice brightened. "Tomorrow afternoon I'll come and sit with Chantalene so you can get out for a while. I'm sure you have things to do, and it'll be a break for me, too."

There was no way to argue. "Okay. I do need to get glass for this broken window of hers. And mine."

"Good. See you tomorrow."

After he'd hung up, he heard movement in the bedroom and found Chantalene sitting up on the edge of her bed, her scratch-marked face pale with exertion.

"What do you think you're doing?"

"I'm going to use that attractive urinal, if you'll please hand it to me and leave the room," she said.

"Oh. Sure."

He closed the door and stood in the hall.

"Get away from there!" she called.

"Okay, I'm going. Yell if you need something."

He went into the kitchen and looked in the refrigerator. Some of the stuff inside he didn't even recognize. In the freezer, he found homemade lasagna with something green inside. He put it in the oven anyway. Tomorrow in El Rio he'd get groceries, including some good old, cholesterol-laden, red meat. And a twelve-pack of beer. His stomach rumbled at the thought.

When Chantalene hadn't called in a few minutes, he tapped on the door. "Finished?"

"Yes." It sounded like a groan.

She was lying back on the bed, her body discreetly covered, but her cast hung over the side onto the floor. "I can't lift the damned thing," she said miserably.

He helped her as gently as he could. "I'll empty your bottle. Where is it?" he said.

Red splotches bloomed like roses on her white face. "I hid it under the bed."

"Stop being embarrassed," he ordered. "Everyone has bodily functions. Speaking of which, how hot should I set the oven for heating up frozen lasagna?"

An hour later, he placed two plates on a tray and carried them to her room. He'd made garlic bread and a salad and felt proud of his efforts. Not bad for a meatless meal.

Chantalene's appetite had returned, a good sign, and between them they polished off the pasta and a couple of wine coolers he'd found in the back of the pantry. She had refused her pain medication, so he figured the cooler wouldn't hurt.

Afterward, he set the trays aside and dealt gin rummy on the bedspread. She didn't take much interest until he beat her three hands in a row. When she unwound the bandage from her wrist and threw the brace in a corner so she could deal, he knew she was going to be all right.

By ten o'clock, though, she looked tired. Tucking her in for the night, he indulged a quick vision of slipping the red t-shirt off over her head and crawling in beside her.

Instead, he said good night and slunk off to his lonely bed on the sofa.

He was sleeping the comatose sleep of the innocent when a sharp *thwack* brought him awake—almost. With his eyes still closed, the sound took him back to the rented house he'd once shared with three other law students, where the newspaper hit the metal storm door in the pre-dawn darkness every day, a signal he had one more hour to sleep. He smiled.

But whose damned dog was barking?

He opened his eyes to total darkness, with no idea where he was. Then the mingled odors of licorice and lasagna reminded him, and he heard a sub-conscious memory of the *thwack* against the front door.

He sat up, scanning the darkness.

"Drew?" Chantalene called from the bedroom.

"I'm up."

"What was that noise?"

"I'll check it out." He went to the front door and stepped outside. The porch felt cool beneath his bare feet.

Except for Bones' barking, the night was quiet and moonless with a damp southwesterly breeze. He looked down the driveway, saw nothing; listened, but heard nothing.

Bones circled warily around a small, dark object on the porch, growling as she stepped close enough to sniff at it, barking as she retreated. Her neck hair rolled forward in a ruff.

"Easy, girl. Let's see what you've got."

He picked up a brown paper bag the size of a lunch sack. It was tied at the neck with twine and contained something solid, but not heavy. He searched the night landscape again. If someone had been here, he must have parked on the road and come up the driveway on foot, and caught Bones sleeping. Drew took the bag inside and turned on the light.

"Drew, are you there? What's happening?" Chantalene's voice sounded frantic.

"I'm here," he called. "Everything's all right."

"If you don't tell me what's going on, I'm coming out there!"

"Okay, okay. Stay put." Reluctantly, he carried the paper bag to her bedroom. "Somebody left us a gift. Or else Bones found it somewhere."

Chantalene had switched on the bedside lamp. She eyed the sack and frowned. "Bones didn't throw it against the front door," she said pointedly. "What is it?"

"I don't know. It sure stinks."

He loosened the twine knot and peeked inside the sack. And saw feathers. Not wanting to reach inside, he crouched and dumped the contents of the sack onto the floor close to the lamp.

"Jeez," Chantalene said, leaning over the edge of the bed. "What is it?"

"The head of a chicken."

He picked up a loose end of twine that had been fashioned around the chicken's neck like a hangman's noose. Wrinkled lids, near translucent, covered the dried-up eyes. The neck felt stiff but the red comb hung limp as wilted lettuce.

"Rhode Island Red," Chantalene said. "Opal Bond."

"What?"

"Opal Bond's the only one around here who raises Rhode Island Red chickens."

He nodded. "I remember seeing those bronze-colored chickens when I went out there."

"You went out there?"

He shrugged it off and picked up three other items that had fallen from the sack. The stub of a candle, a slip of paper, and a tiny pocketknife. "What the hell is this stuff?" He laid the candle and knife on the bedspread and opened the paper.

The message was printed in block letters, backhanded as if to disguise the writing. *"Sins of the parents are visited upon the children. Get out while you can,"* he read.

He glanced up, but Chantalene didn't react to the message. She was fingering the small pocketknife, turning it over in the palm of her hand.

Her voice was a whisper. "This was my father's knife."

Drew sat beside her on the bed and looked at the pearl-handle of the knife, stained with age. "My dad used to have one of those, too. How can you tell it was your father's?" She held it beneath the lamp and opened the longer of its two blades. She pointed to the tip, which was broken off at a ragged angle. "I did that. I was trying to break open a piece of quartz rock I'd found, to see what it looked like inside. I wasn't supposed to be playing with his knife, and I had to do the dishes by myself for a week." Her smile looked tortured. "Daddy carried this in his pocket everywhere he went. He would have had it with him when he died."

Drew frowned, anger clotting in his chest. "It can't be Little Willie this time. He's still in jail."

"No. But I'll bet he's the one who stole the knife from my father's body." She swallowed. "This is too subtle for Willie, anyway," she said, picking up the candle stub. "This is Opal's work. The candle is probably a witchcraft symbol. The dead chicken, too. Maybe I've been underestimating Opal all this time."

"What about Big Willie?"

Chantalene shook her head. "I don't know. He could have threatened to talk to me. Or maybe she'd just had enough of his bullying."

"I can't see Opal killing anybody," Drew said. "She might skulk around in the night, delivering warnings, but she's too meek to commit murder."

"I never thought of her as violent, either. But then I never really knew her. Nobody does." She picked up the note. "*Sins of the parents are visited upon the children.* I wonder whose sins she blamed for Berta Jean's retardation."

Drew thought about that. "Maybe her husband's?"

She met his eyes. "Opal wouldn't necessarily have to do the killing herself. She might have more influence on her son than anybody suspects."

Does a mother have that much influence over a son? Drew wondered. Would I kill if my mother had asked me to? If my father had beaten her?

Who could know what went through the mind of a man like Little Willie Bond?

He gathered up the candle, note and chicken head and put them back in the sack. Chantalene handed him the knife.

"I'll take these to Sheriff Justin tomorrow and see if he can trace the note. For tonight, though, I'm damned glad Little Willie isn't on the loose." Drew sealed the brown bag inside a plastic one and put it in the freezer, but the aroma of dead chicken clung to the house.

Lying awake on the sofa the rest of the night, he traced out the hours on the cracks in the ceiling, acutely aware of the warning. He was sure that Chantalene, too, lay sleepless in the haunted dark.

The next morning, she seemed stronger, the line of her chin more determined. Right or wrong, Drew decided that focusing guilt on a flesh-and-blood villain was good for her. He brought her juice and cereal for breakfast, then carried her to a chair on the front porch where she directed his chores.

He tethered Whippoorwill near a patch of fresh grass outside his corral, measured the front window for glass, picked tomatoes from the garden. The air was thick with humidity and warming up fast. Though she wouldn't admit it, he could tell Chantalene's leg was hurting when he carried her back inside. He saw the lines around her eyes and the clench of her lips whenever she moved. He put her in bed and refused to let her up again unless she swallowed a pain pill. She called him a name, but she finally took it.

In early afternoon, Martha Jenks parked her Buick in front of the house. Drew met her on the porch with a finger over his lips.

"She's dozing," he said.

Martha modulated her vigorous voice. "That's good. Come carry some of this food, will you?"

She had brought two boxes draped with clean terry dishtowels. Both were heavy and smelled great. He carried them into the kitchen and helped unpack casseroles, fried chicken, apple pie, and brownies, salivating while he gave Martha a running commentary of instructions on convalescent care.

Finally, she turned to him and smiled. "We'll be fine, Drew. I've done this before."

"Right." He smiled, feeling stupid. "You're a nurse. Sorry."

His smile faded when he remembered where she'd been that morning. "How was the funeral?" Lame question. "I mean, did everything go all right?"

"The church overflowed," Martha said. Her eyes looked tired. "Monkey and Slim don't have any family left, but neighbors I haven't seen in years showed up. Thelma must have phoned the whole state. Even Opal Bond came out. I couldn't believe it."

"I can. Opal gets around." He told her about their unseen visitor in the night, and the grisly gift he planned to deliver to Sheriff Justin that day. But not that they suspected Opal of murder.

Martha made a face. "Sounds like something Opal might dream up, all right."

"I hate to leave you two alone out here," he said.

"Don't be silly. With Little Willie in jail, Opal's no danger to anyone except herself. She won't show up, but even if she did, I can handle Opal Bond."

He bet she could, at that. When he retold the incident in daylight, the chicken's head and note seemed more childish than ominous. But at least he'd warned her.

Martha opened the refrigerator and took inventory with a glance. "Um, mum." She shook her head. "You two could starve to death on what's in here. Where's your shopping list?"

She dictated a list of groceries and he wrote them down. Martha had a way of putting things in perspective. He felt both foolish and relieved.

Now if Sheriff Justin could match the handwriting on the note to Opal and bring her in for questioning, perhaps the whole ugly mystery of Chantalene's lost family would be solved. And prove, Drew hoped fervently, that his father had nothing to do with it.

# SIXTEEN

*Three stunned leghorns, their white wings unfurled, glassy eyes blinking, hung upside down from Mama's hands. She thrust a pair of chicken feet towards Chantalene. "Take this one. Don't think about it. Just do it. You've got to learn."*

*The spurs on the chicken's bony feet scratched her wrist. She swung the pullet over and under, over and under in a wide circle, the way Mama had shown her. After six swings, her arm aching, she laid the senseless chicken on the ground and placed her foot on its neck.*

*She hesitated.*

Somewhere outside the dream, voices sifted through Chantalene's subconscious: a man's voice, safe and comforting. And a woman's that melded with the dream.

*"Pull! Pull hard! Don't make it suffer!"*

*Chantalene shifted her weight onto the pullet's neck and pulled with all her might.*

The dream jumped backwards like an old movie reel.

*"Chantalene! Come here and help me. We've got to get six dressed by noon for the Allisons to pick up." Mama thrust the bony chicken feet into her hands.*

*But Mama's voice had changed.*

*Chantalene looked at her—and it wasn't Mama at all.*

*It was Martha Jenks.*

She jerked awake, sweating. Her fractured leg throbbed and the sheet beneath her felt hot. She shifted in the bed, but the heavy cast didn't move and the effort made her leg hurt worse.

Voices drifted to her from the kitchen—Drew and Martha, talking softly, trying not to wake her.

It was Martha in the dream. Not Mama. That was why the dream always felt distorted.

Lying in the steamy nest of her bed, she remembered the first months she stayed with the Jenkses. Martha raised fryers for sale to the neighbors. Chantalene had forgotten Martha's efforts to teach her how to kill and dress chickens.

She closed her eyes and saw Martha's foot clamped behind the chicken's head as the bloody neck cords pulled free. A nauseating mass swelled in her stomach.

Why would that dream haunt her all these years? Why hadn't she remembered it was Martha? Thank god it was white chickens in the dream, not red like the one delivered to her front porch last night.

She heard Drew getting ready to leave for El Rio. Even though she'd known Martha was coming, she now felt unnerved about being alone with her.

In the living room, the screen door squeaked open. Was he leaving already?

"Drew!" Her voice was hoarse and had no volume. The screen slapped shut and his footsteps descended the porch steps. The car door slammed, the motor roared, and he was gone.

She lay rigid in the bed, alarm ringing in her ears.

It was only a dream, she told herself. Martha would be possessive and bossy but no different from how she'd always been. Chantalene counted her breaths as she waited for Martha to appear in the doorway. It didn't take long.

"You're awake!" Martha plopped her canvas tote bag beside the black rocking chair. She leaned over the bed and smiled. "How's the patient today?"

Chantalene swallowed. "Okay. Just tired."

Martha touched her forehead. Her fingers felt cool and rough as a man's. "You're all clammy. We'll get you a nice warm sponge bath." Martha smiled again, happy to be fussing over her.

"Don't bother. They bathed me yesterday at the hospital, and I haven't done much to get dirty."

"Nonsense! You'll feel lots better when you're fresh and clean. You'll see. Besides, we certainly can't leave it for Drew to do, can we?"

Chantalene did feel sticky and in need of washing, but she cringed at the thought of Martha's hands on her body. "Maybe later."

Martha patted her sheet-covered knee. "No time like the present! I'll get a basin of warm water." She strode from the room.

Years of resentment rushed back to Chantalene. She was twelve years old, forced by that same tone of voice to attend church wearing the dress Martha had bought her instead of her own clothes. The dress was green and blue plaid and Chantalene hated it. After that she'd refused to wear anything but red and black—like her mother.

Martha returned with a wash cloth and towel, soap and a dishpan of water. "Let's get you out of that shirt."

Martha's hands were cold as a corpse. Chantalene flinched.

"Sorry, dear," Martha said, immersing the washcloth in the yellow dishpan. "Back when we had a milk cow, Monkey wouldn't let me do the milking because of my cold hands. Said it would be dangerous for me and torture for the cow." She chuckled.

Stripped, Chantalene sat up as best she could, a captive to her foster mother's ministrations. She held up her hair while Martha soaped her back. Why had she let Martha bully her into this? If she had thrown a tantrum like a child, would the woman have held her down and washed her against her will?

*Stop over-reacting.* She quelled her frustration, tried not to think about Martha's hands. "How's Monkey doing? I was worried about him the other day."

Martha sighed. "So was I. He'd watched out for Slim all his life, and he took it hard. But Monkey's strong. He'll bounce back."

As Chantalene remembered it, Martha was the one who'd always watched out for Slim, but she didn't say so.

Wind rattled the guttering outside her bedroom window and a cloud shadow crossed the room. The curtains puffed inward.

"Storm coming," Martha said. Something mournful in her tone raised goose bumps on Chantalene's bare skin.

Martha smoothed the washcloth over her shoulders and lower back. "Such a beautiful girl. You always were."

Chantalene's chest tightened. She was not imagining things; there was something distinctly haywire about Martha.

"I'll do the rest myself," she said, taking the washcloth from Martha's hands.

The rain started with huge, slow drops that splattered audibly against the house, isolating them in the small room with an unwelcome intimacy. She finished her bath awkwardly while Martha watched, balancing the pan on the bed so it wouldn't spill. Martha's gaze slipped over her body, following every stroke of the cloth.

"I always wished you were my real daughter," Martha said. "Did you know I delivered you?"

"Yes. Mama told me."

Martha's face darkened. "Your father wouldn't take LaVita to the hospital, because he didn't want anyone ...

*looking* at her. Can you imagine?" She shook her head. "And he didn't have the guts to help her himself. He went into town and drank himself senseless while she lay out here alone in labor."

Chantalene knew her father wasn't a paragon of courage, but Martha's criticism still irritated her. "Mama probably ran him out of the house," she said, lightly. "In the Gypsy culture, men aren't allowed to attend a birth."

Martha didn't seem to hear. Her eyes had taken on a faraway look that sent another flash of goose bumps over Chantalene.

"Luckily, Monkey saw Clyde in town that day," Martha said. "He made enough sense out of Clyde's drunken ramblings to know LaVita needed help, and he called me. Then he kept Clyde occupied while I came over. If I hadn't, you both might have died."

Or LaVita might have delivered me by herself just fine, Chantalene thought. But she couldn't imagine being left to experience childbirth alone, and the whole unfathomable mystery of her eccentric parentage surged up in her chest, choking off further defense of her father. Outdoors, the guttering rattled again. The humid air felt heavy and overly warm.

"You were born right here in this room," Martha said. She glanced at the walls as if they might confirm the story. "With a full head of black hair and screaming like a meat saw."

Startled at the image, Chantalene glanced up and met Martha's eyes. It was like looking at a one-way mirror. No way to know what was going on behind them.

Why was Martha telling her this stuff today? In all the months Chantalene had lived with the Jenkses, Martha refused to talk about Chantalene's parents, changing the subject if someone else mentioned them.

A splinter of memory arose. "Martha," she said slowly, "the day after my mother left, she called on the phone. You thought I was asleep and didn't tell me until later, and I remember being really angry." She paused. "What did she say to you that day?"

Martha paused, the glow of nostalgia dissolving from her face. She shrugged. "I told you then. She said she had to go away because she thought someone wanted to kill her."

For a moment the mirror behind Martha's eyes cleared, betraying the lie. "No, she didn't," Chantalene said. "I know she thought someone wanted to kill her, and obviously she was right. But she'd never have run away without me."

Thunder rattled the windows. An ozone-scented breeze swept through the window and Martha moved quickly to shut out the rain.

Chantalene grabbed the towel and wrapped it around her torso. When Martha came back to the bed, her face wore a mask of compassion. "Honey, I know finding your mother's body was upsetting, but it's time you accepted the fact that LaVita *did* abandon you."

"Did she?" Anger sharpened Chantalene's voice. "You were gone from the house several hours that evening." Martha leaving her alone, saying she had to visit a sick friend in El Rio. Monkey, coming in from the field, frowning when Chantalene told him. The two of them eating supper in silence. "You met her, didn't you? You saw her that day!"

Martha shook her head. "Let it go, child. Stop tormenting yourself." She brushed a strand of Chantalene's hair behind her shoulder. "I'll clean up the bath things and fix your hair. I could braid it for you, so it won't get so tangled." She laid a clean t-shirt on the bed and carried the basin away.

Chantalene shivered despite the stuffiness of the room now that the window was closed. She yanked the clean shirt over her head and tucked the sheet around her waist.

Martha *had* seen her mother that day; she was sure of it.

Her mind flashed to the night LaVita left her on Martha's front porch ... Martha pushing open the screen door, her long braid swinging down in front of her nightgown ...

In all the time Chantalene stayed there, she'd never seen Martha go to bed without brushing out her hair. She re-braided it every morning.

Perhaps that night she'd hadn't had time to brush out her hair ... because she'd only gotten home a few minutes before LaVita and Chantalene arrived.

She glanced at Martha's tote bag beside the chair. What, besides her embroidery, did Martha carry in that bag? Her heart beat fast as the rain against the window. She scanned the room for a weapon—something she could hide beneath the sheet.

Instead, she saw on the floor beneath her desk a piece of yellow paper, with one torn corner. Her breath lodged in her throat.

Her sketch of the four hangmen!

It had fallen from Drew's hands the morning she caught him snooping and now it lay only a few feet from the rocking chair. If Martha saw it, she would know Chantalene had been at the scene of her father's murder.

*She smelled the October wind, felt the dry grass scratch her ankles. She watched the four dark figures hurry from the haybarn toward the road. The bulk and gait of the first one was familiar—Big Willie Bond. And behind him the tall, thin form of Slim Jenks. Then a voice, tinged with hysteria—Little Willie's! The others silent, ominous.*

*Something was odd about the last figure. The walk*

*seemed familiar, but not like a man's. White shoes in the moonlight ...*

The memory scalded her eyes. Her mouth opened and a small, strangled sound escaped. *Martha Jenks!*

She had to keep Martha from seeing that drawing. The woman was worse than haywire; she was homicidal. If she knew Chantalene suspected her, Sheriff Justin would find her body in a cellar, too.

Every day for the last ten years, she'd sworn never to be helpless again. Now here she sat, weighted to this bed like a chained animal. She couldn't even run!

She threw back the sheet and hoisted her cast over the edge of the bed. The leg throbbed and her hands shook.

She could hear Martha running water in the bathroom. Holding onto the footboard, she pushed herself upright and tried putting weight on her broken leg. A lightning bolt streaked up her thigh.

She gritted her teeth, waited, then tried again.

This time she knew what to expect. She steeled herself and searched the room. Where were those damned crutches they'd brought home from the hospital? She spotted them leaning against the chest of drawers on the opposite side of the bed. Too far away to help her now.

She turned toward the desk and tried one shaky step without turning loose of the bedpost. Even her good leg trembled at the knee and threatened to fold.

The toilet flushed.

She dropped back onto the bed and edged off onto the floor. In a sitting position, butt first, she pulled herself across the floor with her hands. The sketch lay only a few feet away.

A gust of rain slammed into the window, pushing her heart into her throat. *Drag, pull. Drag, pull.* The cast felt like an anvil and pinched her hip; the carpet scraped her skin. One more pull and she could stretch out on the floor and grab the paper.

She sprawled and extended.

Her fingers snaked between the legs of the desk and grasped the sketch. She clutched it to her pounding chest. Eyes closed, she wished for the supernatural powers her superstitious neighbors attributed to her and aimed a telepathic message toward Drew Sander: *Come back, Drew. I need help!*

"My word, child! What are you doing?"

Her eyes flew open.

Martha, no small woman at eye level, loomed above her, stories tall. Her khaki pantlegs stretched up like totem poles, crimps at the knees forming hideous smiles.

Chantalene tugged her shirttail down, tucking the sketch into the top of her cast.

"I fell," she said. "But I'm all right. No harm done."

Martha frowned and her eyes darkened. "I didn't hear you fall. What's that you've got?"

She reached for the paper, but Chantalene snatched the sketch first.

With a motion as casual as stepping on a bug, Martha's foot pinned her wrist to the floor. She pried the paper from Chantalene's fingers and opened it.

"What's this? A drawing?"

Chantalene's pulse pounded as she watched Martha's eyes travel over the sketch, her lips pronouncing each set of initials.

"Oh," Martha said slowly. "I see."

Chantalene cried out as the white nurse's shoe clamped down on her wrist so hard she thought the bone would snap. She closed her eyes and saw the death dance of the headless chicken.

# SEVENTEEN

When the dusty red roads were behind and only blacktop lay between him and El Rio, Drew rolled down the car windows. The wind smelled of Indian summer and washed him with nostalgia. For the first time in two weeks, he felt comfortable, as if he were finally home.

Tension drained from his limbs, replaced by fatigue. He hadn't had a normal night's sleep since his first day back, when he'd lain on his sleeping bag in his parents' old farmhouse and listened to the cicadas' song of summer from the elms. In lieu of sleep, he promised himself a couple of beers and an old-fashioned, greasy hamburger before he headed back to Tetumka. With Chantalene safely in Martha's care, he didn't have to hurry.

He thought about Little Willie Bond in the El Rio jail, and Opal Bond skulking through the night to throw her gruesome warning on Chantalene's front porch. What kind of genes produced a family like that? Undoubtedly Chantalene was right about the father and son being members of the lynch team twelve years ago. But unless Opal or Little Willie admitted it, how could it ever be proven?

He glanced at his watch. First he'd stop at the builders' supply and leave his window measurements, again. Then he'd go to Sheriff Justin's office and show him the contents of the brown paper bag that now sat on the seat beside him, sealed in a plastic zipper-bag. He'd tell the sheriff they suspected Opal, urge him to bring her in for questioning. Perhaps the mother and son had plotted together to rid themselves of Big Willie's tyranny. If she talked, maybe the sheriff could sweat a confession out of Little Willie and put the two of them where they belonged.

Sheriff Justin wasn't in. The young deputy manning the office looked at Drew and smiled. "You don't remember me, do you?" he said.

Drew shrugged an apology. "You do look familiar."

"I'm Duke Ethridge's kid brother."

*"Bobby?"* Drew had graduated from high school with Duke, nick-named for his imitations of John Wayne. Drew and Duke used to lead Bobby into mischief just to see the surprise on his face when he got caught.

Drew pumped his hand. "You, a police officer? My god, what's the world coming to."

Bobby laughed. "Incredible, isn't it? I don't believe it myself."

But his appearance belied his words. Bobby's smile was confident and he looked like a prizefighter in his uniform, not over-muscled, but iron hard. He was still a couple inches shorter, but Drew wouldn't have risked playing tricks on him now.

"Where's Duke these days?"

"Up in Oklahoma City, working at the racetrack. You wound up in New York, didn't you?"

"Yeah. Go figure. What's he do at the track?"

"Loses money, mostly." Bobby grinned. "But he's single. He can get by with that."

"You're married?"

"Yes, sir. Wife and two little girls."

"Wow," Drew said, and heard envy in his voice. Bobby must have heard it, too; his smile widened.

"You moving back to the farm?" Bobby asked.

"No. Or yes." Drew shrugged again. "Temporarily, I guess."

"Can't decide whether you're an Okie or a New Yorker, huh?"

"That's about it. Right now I'm a native of the state of flux." Drew wanted off that subject. "Any idea when Sheriff Justin will be in?"

"By three, at least. That's when I get off."

Less than an hour away. "Will you see that he gets this sack? Trust me, you don't want to look inside. I've already phoned him about it. I'll check back later."

"Sure thing."

Drew paused at the door. "Where's the best place in town to get a beer and a burger?"

"Pancho's," Bobby said, without hesitation. "Three blocks down, one block over. Great nachos, too."

Drew saluted. "Maybe I'll see you there."

"It's a definite possibility."

An afternoon thunderstorm was brewing and the air smelled of ozone. Dry leaves scuttled across the sidewalk as Drew parked across the street from Pancho's. Neon brand names lit the window of the storefront bar.

Only three other vehicles were within sight, one of them a familiar blue pickup. He peeked into the cab and shook his head. It was Monkey's, all right. This was the last place he'd have expected to find him, though God knew after what the old farmer had been through today, he was entitled to a few beers.

Inside Pancho's, Drew paused while his eyes adjusted to the dusty gloom. Wooden tables on iron pedestals scattered out on either side of a scuffed path to the bar. At a table near the front, a domino game was in progress. No player was under seventy. They glanced up in unison when he walked past, but nobody spoke. Neither did Monkey Jenks, who sat at a back table by himself, his big shoulders curled over a long-necked brown bottle.

The dark-skinned woman tending bar greeted him with a smile. Her beautiful face seemed too small for a body that barely fit between the counter and the backbar. Duke Ethridge would have said, in his JW drawl, "I'd like to buy her by the head and sell her by the pound." A radio played country and western, but not too loud.

He ordered a burger and carried his beer over to Monkey's table. Four empty bottles sat in the center. "Rather be left alone?" Drew said.

Monkey glanced up with blank eyes, then went back to contemplating his beer. "Suit yourself."

He dragged up a chair, wondering what to say to a man who'd just buried his brother. He took a drink and didn't say anything, letting Garth Brooks fill in the silence. The beer was ice cold and Drew took a moment to enjoy its slide down his throat. And since Okie beer was only 3.2, he could have another and still be okay to drive.

He might need to drive Monkey home, as well. He'd never seen the man like this.

"Sorry I couldn't make the funeral," Drew said finally. "Martha said it was packed."

Monkey looked up, blinked. "You talked to Martha?"

Drew nodded. Monkey tipped up his bottle, then set it carefully back into the wet ring on the tabletop. "She'll miss him more'n anybody, I reckon. Slim had a crush on her since high school." Monkey's drawl had magnified under the influence, but the glaze in his blue eyes went deeper than mere intoxication. "He'd of done anything for her."

Drew's neck hairs rose up like antennae.

Monkey drained his beer and lifted the bottle, but not his eyes, toward the bar.

"Coming up," the bartender called.

Monkey set the bottle carefully alongside the others in the center of the table. "Guilt finally got him," he mumbled.

Before Drew could ask him to repeat, the wooden floor vibrated with the approach of the bartender/waitress. She set a burger in a plastic mesh basket in front of Drew and a fresh beer before Monkey, without bothering to clear away the empties.

"Chantalene okay?" Monkey asked suddenly.

"Yeah, she's at home."

Monkey shook his head. "Wish to hell she'd stayed in Ada. Slim'd still be alive."

The French fries were sizzling, and the aroma of grease and mustard made Drew's mouth water. But his throat had constricted so tightly he couldn't swallow. Monkey was telling him something—without telling him.

Drew pushed the burger basket from in front of him and leaned both arms on the table, giving Monkey his full attention. He waited.

"I just looked the other way," Monkey mumbled. "Didn't want to admit what I knew."

Drew could see the booze was loosening a secret too painful for Monkey to deal with sober. And too heavy to carry any longer.

"Knew what, Monkey?" Drew didn't want to hear it, but he had to.

Monkey wagged his head, and an edge of bitterness hardened his drawl. "It's all on her daddy's head, the *bastard!* All the dead ones. He ruined her when she was just a little girl. She couldn't hate her own father, but she'd never love or trust another man."

Drew frowned. "Chantalene?"

Monkey ignored him. "I didn't know about it till the old man died," he said, "long after we were married. If I'da known, I guess I'da killed him." His voice faded and Drew leaned forward until their heads were only inches apart.

*"Martha's father?"*

Was that what Monkey was saying? Drew thought of that brooding photograph in Martha's living room, and her comment about her father's lies.

Monkey hugged his elbows on the tabletop and began a barely perceptible rocking motion. He looked up at Drew with tears in his eyes, and in pained, confused voice whispered: "The day she agreed to marry me, she told me I reminded her of her dad."

Monkey turned his head and vomited beer on the floor.

Drew heard the bartender swear, and then the clatter of a mop handle and her heavy steps approaching. Monkey slumped over on the table, head on his folded arms.

Drew frowned, astounded by Monkey's confession. But what was he confessing?

If Martha's father had abused her, how was that connected to Slim's death, or to Chantalene?

Everything he knew about Montgomery Jenks contradicted the notion that he was capable of anything unkind, let alone evil. Monkey even refused to shoot coyotes back in the days when farmers lined the fences with the predators' ears. Drew's dad had said Monkey wouldn't even kill a chicken for Sunday dinner; he couldn't put down his old horse when it broke a leg in a prairie dog hole. Martha had to do it.

*I looked the other way. Didn't want to admit what I knew.*

*He'd of done anything for her.*

The stuffy air of the bar grew thick and buzzed around him. His chair raked backwards and tipped over as he came to his feet.

"Where's the phone?" he yelled at the startled bar maid.

She nodded toward a pay phone on the wall. He ran for it, digging in his pocket for a quarter.

Squeezing the earpiece, he listened to the futile ringing of Chantalene's phone. Six, seven, eight rings. Martha wasn't picking up.

Daylight flashed into the bar as the outside door opened, then closed again.

*Eleven, twelve, thirteen ...*

Bobby Ethridge, disarmed but still in uniform, ambled to the bar and ordered a beer, then turned and waved to him. *Fourteen, fifteen ...*

Drew slammed down the receiver and threw a wad of bills on the bar as he ran past, catching Bobby's arm and dragging him along. "Come on. We've got to go."

"What the hell ... "

"Where's your squad car? I'll explain on the way!"

# EIGHTEEN

Over the drumming of the rain and her own heartbeat, Chantalene heard the robotic trill of the kitchen phone.

If Martha heard it, too, she showed no sign. Her eyes were fixed on the sketch of four hooded vigilantes.

Chantalene's hand felt numb where Martha's foot clamped her wrist to the floor. She braced herself for Martha's rage or alarm, but instead her face sagged with a sudden aging. She looked down on her captive with sorrow in her eyes.

"Chantalene, Chantalene," she crooned. "If only you'd left it alone. If you hadn't come back to Tetumka and stirred things up." Martha stuffed the drawing in her pocket and stepped over Chantalene's cast.

Chantalene flinched as Martha reached down and hooked her hands beneath her arms. With a powerful heave, Martha hoisted Chantalene's torso onto the bed like a side of beef.

"Aaahh!" Pain knifed through Chantalene's leg and sent nausea through her stomach.

Martha scooped up Chantalene's cast along with her good leg and dumped them onto the mattress. Chantalene bit her lip and scrambled to cover herself as if the sheet could protect her.

Martha slumped into the rocking chair. She laid her head back and began to rock with short, determined strokes. The glazed look in her eyes terrified Chantalene more than if she'd been angry.

"It had to be done," Martha said, rocking. "Had to be done." Her voice sounded thick, like someone underwater.

"What had to be done?" Get her talking, stall her until Drew gets back. Chantalene sent him another prayer: *Drew, come home!*

But there was no answer. This reckoning was hers and Martha's alone.

Her foster-mother's hands gripped the arms of the chair, her eyes focused in mid-air. "From the moment you were born," Martha said, "I knew it wasn't safe to leave you in that house. But what could I do? He was your father. And then he raped poor Berta Bond."

"He didn't! Someone else confessed to that!"

Martha ignored her. "I knew what he was doing to you. And I understood why you couldn't stop him." Her voice turned sad. "Little girls always love their fathers."

Chantalene shook her head, knowing even as she spoke that her words couldn't reach Martha. "You're wrong! He never molested me. Why would you think that?"

Martha's feet pushed the rocker with jerky strokes. "After Berta was attacked, I had to do something. I couldn't let it go on. I knew LaVita wouldn't believe you, even if you told her. Just the way my mother wouldn't believe me."

"My God ... "

"It was up to me to save you. To save all the little girls."

Understanding rolled over Chantalene in a sickening wave. "Your father abused you," she whispered, "and you took your revenge on mine."

Martha didn't answer.

Rain pounded the window and a cavernous despair engulfed Chantalene. "But why my mother, Martha? What happened to her?"

Against the black rocking chair Martha's face looked translucent. Her rocking became more agitated, tossing her head with the motion.

"I hadn't planned to harm LaVita," she said. "I thought she would take you and run away after we hanged Clyde. But LaVita was so excitable. You never could predict what she'd do."

Martha smiled. "She brought you to me. Like a gift! I couldn't believe it. Then I realized it was meant to be."

The rocker creaked and her feet kept pushing. Chantalene felt sick.

Martha kept talking, her voice patient and animated, as if she were reading a story to a child. "The next day when LaVita called, she told me she'd seen the men who lynched Clyde and she was going to tell the police. She hadn't recognized me, of course, or she wouldn't have left you with me. I'd kept my face covered and my mouth shut. Not like those stupid Bonds."

Chantalene clenched the sheet in her fists. "*You* killed my mother?"

"I tried to convince her to run away," Martha said, her voice rising. "I told her they'd found a suicide note with Clyde's body. 'It's a lie!' she yelled. 'I saw them lynch him!' 'I believe you,' I told her, 'but nobody else will. Did you give the police any names?' 'Not yet,' she said."

Martha's grip on the chair arms loosened. The rocking slowed to a smooth rhythm. "So I told her they were all covering up for each other, and it was up to us to find some evidence. Otherwise the police would never believe her." She frowned slightly, remembering. "We arranged to meet at dusk north of town, by the boat ramp at Brewer's Lake. We could hide her truck in the trees there and go back to the hay barn to search for clues, I said. Maybe one of the hangmen had dropped something. I told her

I'd bring Monkey's sealed beam light to search with." Her words were deliberate now, as methodical as her terrible plan had been.

Chantalene's throat tightened. Beneath the sheet she inched her cast to the far side of the bed and hooked her ankle over the edge, preparing for escape. For revenge. For anything.

Martha sighed and drew a deep breath. "LaVita was very grateful. 'You're the only friend I have,' she told me. 'But please don't tell Monkey where you're going. I'll explain why when I see you.' That's how I knew she'd recognized Slim."

The rocking slowed and Martha's eyes drooped to narrow slits. "That evening when I pulled up beside the ramp at Brewer's Lake, LaVita's truck was parked in the shadow of the blackjacks. She was upset because I hadn't brought you along, but I told her the less you knew about this the better. I told her we had to think of your safety, and she calmed down."

Chantalene's stomach knotted as she pictured her mother's desperate face.

"She was cold and scared," Martha said, without sympathy, "and she hadn't eaten all day. I gave her the hot chocolate I'd loaded with Benadryl. She drank a whole cup, and I urged her to have another while I drove. She was drowsy even before we reached the pasture, but she never suspected."

Martha rolled her head side to side on the back of the rocking chair, closing her eyes. "By the time we'd climbed the fence and come close to the barn, she was staggering. She never knew what hit her. Didn't even see me pick up the broken fence post. I went back and got the shotgun, to make sure." Her face relaxed now, her work done.

Tears spilled from Chantalene's eyes, but her anguish had turned to rage.

As a child, she'd been powerless to avenge the loss of her parents, but she wasn't powerless now. She glanced at the crutches beside the bureau, a possible weapon, and edged her other leg to the far side of the bed.

Martha relaxed her head against the chair back, her eyes still closed. "I hid the body in the cellar and then I drove to Brewer's lake and pushed her truck into the water. It was the only way." She looked at Chantalene and smiled. "You belonged with me."

Chantalene's tongue felt thick. *Keep her talking.* "What about Big Willie? Was he going to tell me?"

Martha's gaze returned to the past. "He was going to kill you! I knew if the police arrested him, he'd tell everything. Men are so spineless," she said, her voice bitter. "Even Slim. He was loyal, though. He'd never have told."

The rocking chair stopped suddenly. Martha leaned over her tote bag on the floor, digging inside. She came out with a vial and syringe.

"I wish you'd left it alone, but it's too late now," she said, without looking at Chantalene. "You're as stubborn as LaVita."

Martha uncapped the needle and inserted it, inverting the vial with a practiced gesture that roiled Chantalene's blood. Clear liquid filled the syringe.

*Now.*

Chantalene launched herself from the bed, screaming as the cast hit the floor and a current of pain shot through the bone. In her peripheral vision, she saw Martha surge from the chair.

Chantalene lurched two stiff-legged steps toward the crutches, light-headed, pain bolting through her leg. She fought to drag the cast.

Too slow. She crashed to the floor, swearing, just as Martha rounded the bed and sprang for her.

On hands and knee, Chantalene lunged toward the crutches that stood three feet past her outstretched arms. Martha grabbed her right foot and yanked, flooring her. Chantalene screamed.

She rolled onto her back and looked up at her attacker.

Martha watched her eyes as she knelt on Chantalene's feet, anchoring her. In one hand she balanced the syringe upright. The sorrow was gone from her face; her eyes looked hard and righteous. "You should have left things alone."

Chantalene met her eyes and swallowed back a blinding rage. She forced compassion into her voice.

"It's all right, Mother," she whispered. "I understand. Really, I do."

A flicker of confusion crossed Martha's eyes. But she leaned toward Chantalene's right hip with the hypodermic.

Chantalene reached out her arms, made her voice plaintive and small. "Mother? Please hold me. I need you. I need you to protect me."

Martha hesitated. And in that half-second Chantalene crunched her torso forward, locked her hands around the back of Martha's neck and smashed her foster mother's face into her cast.

Martha screamed and dropped the syringe. She clasped both hands over her face, jerking backwards as blood spouted from her nose.

Chantalene rolled away, clenching her teeth against a mind-bending pain.

Martha's scream turned to a roar. On all fours, her chin dripping blood, she crawled after Chantalene and caught her feet. Q

Chantalene lunged for the crutches, missed, caught the open corner of a drawer in the bureau instead, and yanked for all she was worth.

The five-drawer, solid oak bureau teetered forward, balanced for a crazy moment on two legs.

And fell.

It struck Martha squarely on the back of the head. In the instant before it crashed across Chantalene's body, she saw Martha crumple.

Then her own lights flickered, and went out.

# NINETEEN

Raindrops splattered around them as the two men sprinted toward Bobby's patrol car. Drew hesitated when he saw the ten-year-old sedan; his Volvo might go faster. But he wanted the advantage of lights and siren.

He headed for the driver's side but Bobby muscled ahead of him. "No, you don't!"

Drew didn't take time to argue. "Head for Tetumka," he ordered.

"This better be good."

"I think I've left Chantalene Morrell alone with a killer."

They jumped in and Bobby took off. From the inside of the police car, Drew couldn't see the flash of the red strobe light, but he definitely heard the siren. Above its wail and the slap of the windshield wipers, he told Bobby he suspected Martha Jenks was responsible for the murder of Clyde Morrell, and maybe of Big Willie Bond.

"That's preposterous," Bobby shouted back, but he didn't turn off the siren. "We're pursuing Little Willie as a suspect in both cases."

"You may be right, but we can't take the chance. I couldn't grasp it either, until a few minutes ago. Monkey told me Martha's father sexually abused her when she was a child. We studied some cases of child abuse in law school. Sometimes a young girl can't accept hating her father, and in fact, still loves him." Drew's jaw tightened, remembering his visit to Martha's house. "Martha has her father's photograph hanging in her living room."

Bobby grimaced and shook his head. "But the rage has to come out somewhere, is that it?" He slowed up through the last intersection before they hit the highway.

"Exactly," Drew said. "Imagine her sympathy for little Berta Bond when Berta was raped. Martha could have wanted revenge not just for Berta, but for herself."

He knew it was speculation, but he pieced it together aloud. "It wouldn't have been hard to incite the Bond men to lynch Clyde, and Monkey says Slim always did whatever Martha wanted. I'm pretty sure Monkey didn't know about it until later. When he figured it out, he kept quiet because he loved her—and his brother."

"Jesus," Bobby said.

Thunder rumbled overhead as they speared through the rain. Luckily, few other cars were out. Outside of town, Bobby cut the siren but increased his speed. The car lunged up and down over the wavy road like a dolphin through rough waves. Drew braced a hand against the roof to keep his head from hitting.

They neared the Y where the road branched toward Tetumka, and the rain showed no signs of slackening. The car hydroplaned on the curve, the rear wheels swinging toward the ditch. Bobby controlled it with an expertise that made Drew glad Bobby was driving.

The car straightened and gripped the wet road again. "And Chantalene doesn't know all this?" Bobby asked.

"I don't think so. But I'm not sure she'd have told me if she does. And she's reckless enough to ask Martha too many questions." He clenched and unclenched his hands. "I just tried to call from Pancho's and got no answer."

The blacktop evaporated into shale road, but instead of

slowing, Bobby hit seventy-five. The rocky shale provided traction, and the speed helped clear the rain from the windshield.

"There's a short cut to the Morrell place coming up," Drew said, pointing.

Bobby shook his head. "Too muddy."

"Take it! You're a good driver."

"We can't do Chantalene much good if we're stuck!"

Nevertheless, he slowed and took the turn, then gunned it. They hit the red mud and fishtailed. Bobby let up on the gas, twisting the wheel to right the car.

Drew tightened his seat belt and held onto the dashboard. They barreled on, the tires spraying slime, the shrill of Chantalene's unanswered phone echoing in Drew's ears.

With one slippery mile behind them, they plunged into the second, which was worse. Here, dark-colored mud indicated the shale had worn away, and Drew could feel the sucking resistance dragging them down. His heart sank with the tires as they bogged and stalled.

"Damn!" Bobby said. He rocked the car backward and forward, back and forward again. The motor roared and smoked, but the car didn't budge. Stuck.

Drew threw open the door and leaped out, sinking to his shoe tops in muck. Rain soaked his hair and ran into his eyes. Bobby jumped out, too. The car was mired to the axles; no way the two of them could push it out.

They left it there and ran.

# TWENTY

*The dead weight of his body pinned her down. He was so heavy, limber as bagged water.*

*Could this be her daddy? She opened her eyes.*

*Her father's distorted face stared at her, his eyes frozen with terror. She screamed.*

The room shimmered into focus. Chantalene was lying on her stomach, a dull pain throbbing in her left leg and back. She recognized the smell of her red bedroom rug and felt its rough texture pressed against her cheek. Something heavy—breathtakingly heavy—weighted her to the floor. She couldn't breathe. Didn't care. Closed her eyes again.

*Framed against the cavernous dark in the center of the barn, a glowing apparition danced above the floor. Mama's nightgown. A scream caught in her chest. Then she made out the shape of her father's body, a sagging mass, and her mother pressed against him, struggling to hold him while she reached with one arm toward a noose that pulled up on his neck.*

*For a moment, she thought they were suspended there together, hanging from the taut rope. Then she recognized the blocky shapes of hay bales stacked up beneath their feet. Something glinted in her mother's outstretched hand; Mama was trying to cut the rope.*

*She scrambled onto the bales, the dried straw piercing her knees. She braced her feet and held her father's slack body in both arms, pressing her face against his stomach. She smelled his sweat and urine and her mother's rage as she sawed the rope. A terrible hum like a thousand angry bees rose in her mother's throat.*

*Her father's body dropped, toppling the hay bales, knocking all three of them to the dirt floor. The dead weight of him pinned them to the earth.*

*He was so heavy. So very heavy.*

She opened her eyes again, her chest aching.

She remembered. Everything.

She remembered lying on the barn floor in her mother's arms; saw again her father's dark, twisted face; heard Mama's repeated command, "*Don't ever tell anyone what you saw!*" She had followed her mother's order by forgetting.

Sobs shook her chest. In the silent room, her hoarse voice sounded pitiful, but this time she didn't fight the tears. When she'd cried herself out, her vision cleared in ripples. She saw the black-lacquered bureau weighing her down, and reality slammed home.

*Martha! Where was Martha?*

Her breath caught in her throat. She listened; heard nothing but her pulse pounding in her ears and the steady patter of rain against the house.

Inching her head to the right to see past the bureau, she saw Martha's khaki-covered legs stretched out on the floor, motionless. Chantalene strained her neck forward and watched Martha's diaphragm for movement. At first she saw none, then discerned a slight rise and fall beneath the flowered blouse. Martha was unconscious, but alive.

The overturned chest of drawers lay at an angle, propped up by Chantalene's cast but pinning her to the floor. The heavy cast was the only thing that had kept the bureau from crushing her. Martha's face looked ashen, blood oozing from her nose and a gash in her scalp where the bureau had hit her.

What if Martha woke up, and she was still pinned there? Heat flashed through her, so intense she thought her bones would melt into the floor.

Drawn by her perspiration, a housefly buzzed around her head. She thought of the meat case in Bond's Market, and pictured Big Willie's macabre death sprawl.

She shuddered, gagged. When the nausea passed, she pushed both hands between the small of her back and the oak chest, took a breath, and heaved.

Her face mashed into the carpet and her elbows trembled, but the chest didn't move. A claustrophobic fear darkened her vision. She closed her eyes and sucked oxygen.

*Don't panic.*

Her leg, her head, her whole body throbbed. She felt hopeless, pegged to the floor like a wriggling insect.

The fly landed on her upper lip and her face convulsed. *There was an old lady who swallowed a fly* ... Hysterical laughter rose in her throat. *I don't know why she swallowed a fly.*

*Perhaps she'll die.*

But she didn't want to die.

She inhaled and fought to clear her head. Maybe she could inch out from under the chest and crawl away. If she could make it to the living room before Martha woke up, she could hide around the corner, maybe trip her as she came through the door. Use the lamp for a club ...

If only she could turn over onto her back, she'd have a better chance of shoving the heavy bureau off. But when she twisted her torso, her leg twisted, too, and pain shot down to her ankle. She lay panting, but she had moved herself an inch or two beneath the bureau. She set her teeth and tried again.

Another flash of pain, another inch toward propping the bureau up with her hip. Again. And again. Now she could brace her palm on the floor and use one elbow to push against the oak chest. One last lunge and she was on her back, the bureau coming down hard again against the thigh part of the cast. She lay still, panting.

And heard a noise. A foot scraping against the floor. Martha's foot.

Her throat pinched shut. She craned her neck to see Martha's face.

Martha's eyes were still closed, but she must be rousing. That's when Chantalene realized that Martha's head lay beneath the elevated corner of the bureau. If by some miracle she were able to lift the bureau enough to extract her legs, the chest would crash down directly on her foster mother's temple.

The force would kill her.

She took a deep breath and laid her head back on the floor.

She had wanted revenge. Dreamt of revenge. This was her chance.

Did she want Martha to die? Is that how it had to end?

Martha had taken her in, tried to protect her from the evil she perceived in the world. Martha had loved her. And in a way, at least sometimes, Chantalene had loved Martha, too.

But the woman was a murderer. So what if she'd been warped by her own father? She was insane maybe, but criminally insane. If not for Martha, Chantalene would still have her family.

The familiar rage boiled up inside her. She pictured herself heaving the bureau off her cast, pulling the cast free and watching the corner of the huge oak chest crush Martha's head into the floor.

The thought raised a gorge in her throat—but also a cruel sense of satisfaction. Perspiration trickled from her forehead into her hair. She breathed through her mouth. Was she willing to do to Martha what Martha had done to her mother?

Perhaps she was. No one else had to know; she'd say it was self-defense. The idea was sickening, and appealing. But most of all she was sick of the anger that had ruled her life for so many years.

Martha's foot moved again.

She had to act fast. Martha had already proven she had no pangs of conscience about doing in her foster daughter.

Chantalene braced her elbows on the floor and her palms against the black lacquered bureau. Pushing with all her strength, she managed to bend her right knee upward and brace it, too, beneath the bureau. Her broken leg had gone numb, blessedly numb. The pain was gone, but so was her ability to move the cast. The leg was dead weight.

Chantalene took a deep breath and heaved. The top end of the bureau lifted above her. With a huge thrust she swiveled it up and away, kicking out with her good leg, scraping her shin as the bureau turned sideways and crashed to the floor only inches beyond Martha's head.

Martha's eyelashes fluttered. Chantalene rolled over fast and scuttled like a crab down the short hall to the living room. She grabbed the antique flatiron that served as a doorstop and sat up, her back against the wall beside the doorway. She held the flatiron in both hands, shoulder level, and listened, her breath coming hard.

What she heard was Bones' barking and heavy footsteps slogging through the rain.

"Chantalene!"

It was Drew's voice, out of breath, panicky. The sweetest

sound she'd ever heard. His feet pounded on the porch and the door burst open.

She dropped the flatiron and closed her eyes.

When she opened them his rain-streaked face appeared above her like a harvest moon, pale and beautiful. "Chantalene?"

A drop of rainwater slipped from his hair and plopped on her cheek. She snaked out her dry tongue and tried to drink it.

He touched her face. "Are you okay?"

"I am now." Another man burst through the door and Chantalene reached to tug down the tail of her t-shirt. She grabbed Drew's arm. "Martha's unconscious in the bedroom. She's the one ... she tried to kill me!"

"I know," he said, smoothing his hand over her hair. "It's all right. The deputy will take care of her. Sit still and rest."

The two men disappeared into the bedroom and the deputy came out leading Martha Jenks, one arm crooked up behind her back. Her face looked groggy and blank as a wall. She didn't even look at Chantalene as they walked past. Chantalene watched the deputy lead Martha to a chair in the kitchen and handcuff her arms behind it. She heard him on the phone calling Sheriff Justin.

Chantalene leaned back and let relief dissolve her bones. It was over.

Drew knelt beside her, his face full of concern. "How badly are you hurt?"

Now that she was safe, every nerve ending in her body had come back to life, screaming. "I hurt all over," she groaned.

"The cast is intact," he said, running his hand over it. "If nothing else is broken, I'll lift you onto the bed." His fingers gently explored her other leg. "Does this hurt?"

"Umm. A little higher and to the left, please."

"You are wicked and indecent," he said, the color returning to his face as he smiled. "I like that in a woman."

He slipped his arms under her knees and shoulders and struggled to his feet. He carried her back to the bedroom and deposited her safely on the rumpled bed. It had never felt so soft and welcome. She closed her eyes, still feeling a dreamlike buzz, and let fatigue wash over her.

Drew brought her a pain pill and a glass of water. She swallowed it gratefully. He straightened the bedclothes and covered her. "My car's in El Rio and Bobby's is stuck in the mud," he said. "I'm sending for an ambulance to take you to the hospital and get you checked over. No arguments."

She didn't try. He left the room and she heard the deputy on the phone again requesting an ambulance, and warning them not to take the unpaved shortcut. By the time Drew came in again, the medication was working and she felt sleepy.

"Where's Martha?"

"Still handcuffed in the kitchen. I'm not sure she even recognizes me."

His expression looked sheepish, as if he still had trouble picturing matronly Martha as a murderer. He hadn't seen Martha in action the way she had, or glimpsed the madness in her eyes.

"Sheriff Justin is on his way," he said. "Try to rest."

Her body wanted sleep, but her nerves jangled. She felt dizzy when she closed her eyes. "You're not leaving, are you?"

He sat on the bed beside her and his warmth felt like sunlight on her skin. His eyes looked bright with worry and, she was fairly sure, something more.

"I'm not going anywhere," he said, "I promise." Leaning down, he placed a light, brief kiss on her mouth.

If she hadn't been so tired, she wouldn't have let him get away with that. She'd have grabbed him and made him kiss her right.

# TWENTY ONE

The rain had stopped by the time Sheriff Justin and the ambulance arrived from El Rio. Chantalene had been dozing, while Drew sat by her bed and the deputy stayed in the kitchen keeping an eye on Martha. She roused when she heard the sheriff's voice directing the deputy to load Martha into the cruiser. Chantalene sat up and Drew propped pillows behind her against the headboard.

The sheriff paused at the door. "May I come in?"

Chantalene met his eyes and hesitated, but only a moment. "Sure," she said. Drew vacated his chair and sat beside her on the edge of the bed.

Sheriff Justin removed his hat. He didn't look tired today. Towering in the doorway, he looked every bit the lawman, but when he spoke, his voice was gentle.

"I'll need you to tell me everything that happened and everything Martha told you," he said. "But first, I owe you an apology."

"Yes," she said. "You do."

The chair creaked when he sat down. "I fell down on my job," he said, his voice low. "I took the obvious conclusion in Clyde's hanging and didn't investigate enough to learn the truth. And I never really tried to find out what happened to your mother. I just assumed she'd run off." He turned his wide-brimmed hat around and around in the big hands. "I'm real sorry for that, Chantalene."

She'd been angry at Sheriff Justin for so many years, why didn't she feel any satisfaction now that he was admitting his mistakes? "It would have helped if I could have remembered what happened that night," she said. "The memory came back to me while ... "

"Wait. I'm not done yet." This time he met her eyes. "I'm sorry for the harsh way I treated you when you kept running away," he said. "I was doin' my job, all right, but I didn't have to be such a hard ass. If I'd listened to you better, maybe I'da figured things out. Or at least made things a little easier on you."

Chantalene had to swallow before she could answer. She traced a pattern in the bedspread with her finger. "You're right that you should have investigated my father's death as a homicide," she said. "But when I was a teenager in trouble, you actually treated me better than I probably deserved. Even then, I thought so."

The sheriff shook his head. "I coulda done better. And I promise you I've learned from those mistakes."

She believed he had. She had never doubted his integrity, just his police work—or lack of it—regarding her father's death.

Sheriff Justin pulled a notebook and pen from the pocket of his windbreaker. "If you're up to it, I'd like to hear the whole story now. Startin' with what you remember about your daddy's hangin'."

She exchanged a look with Drew. "You can do this later if you're too tired," he said, sounding just like an attorney.

"No. I want to get it over with."

She squeezed Drew's hand and began. The telling was cathartic, like laying down a bitter burden. When she was finished, Drew carried her to the ambulance that once again chauffeured her to El Rio Hospital.

# TWENTY TWO

Contradictory emotions lumped in Chantalene's chest as she swung her crutches across the Opalata County Courthouse lawn a week later. She'd waited a long time for justice, and she intended to see it through. But approaching the gray stone building where Martha Jenks' preliminary hearing was set for 10 that morning, her whole body felt as heavy as the cumbersome leg cast.

Beside her, Drew stuffed his hands in his pants pockets and dawdled along at her pace. Century-old oaks dropped bronze leaves on their shoulders, and a crispness in the air made her think of pumpkins and polished apples. For just a moment, she let herself pretend the two of them were simply out for a walk on a day set aside for simple pleasures.

But this was not a day for pleasure.

Sometimes, the anger still burned in her stomach when she considered the damage her former foster-mother had done to so many lives. Yet all morning, forgotten images had haunted her: When she was twelve, Martha had made potato pancakes twice a day because it was the only thing Chantalene would eat. She recalled Martha's anguished eyes the first time she'd run away, and her fierce pride whenever Chantalene brought an A paper home from school.

And, finally, she pictured Martha as a twelve-year-old

girl, defiled in body and spirit by her own father, her life predestined for ruin. Martha's father, like her own, had died young. If he'd lived long enough, would Martha have been able to affix the blame, to settle accounts somehow? And would that have saved Clyde and LaVita Morrell's lives?

Drew put a hand beneath her elbow while she leapfrogged up the courthouse steps. They rode the elevator to the second floor, one flight below the county jail. She pictured Martha occupying the same cell where less than three weeks ago she'd spent a tormented night.

If this was revenge, there was nothing sweet about it.

Courtroom B smelled of furniture polish and old guilt. A half dozen people were scattered among wooden pews. Chantalene chose the fourth row and angled her cast between the benches. Drew propped her crutches against the seat and sat beside her. A constant ache in her leg served as a reminder of her struggle with Martha. She'd had to undergo a second surgery to reset the displaced bone.

Two rows up, Thelma Patterson turned to say hello, her stage whisper clearly audible in the quiet room. Lethargic ceiling fans disseminated Thelma's floral perfume.

A minute later, Monkey Jenks walked in, looking even more like a farmer in his Sunday suit than in his jeans. Silence froze the room and Chantalene's breath caught in her chest. Monkey had been charged as an accessory but released on bond. Without meeting anyone's eyes, he took a seat on the first bench behind the railing and laid his hat on the seat beside him. There was sorrow in the sag of his shoulders and the curve of his neck. Chantalene tightened her jaw and looked at the ceiling.

To one side of the judge's bench, a door squeaked open.

A uniformed officer escorted Martha Jenks toward the defendant's table where her attorney waited. If Chantalene hadn't known the woman so well, she wouldn't have recognized her. Devoid of makeup, her long hair unbraided, Martha looked as haggard and gray as her shapeless jail uniform. Only her posture resembled the woman Chantalene knew. Her straight back and square shoulders sent a wave of resentment through Chantalene. But what had she expected? To see Martha cowering and repentant? Would that have made things right?

Just before she sat down, Martha's glazed eyes flickered across the room with no sign of recognition, until they fell on Monkey. Chantalene caught Martha's wounded expression when a quick look passed between husband and wife, and she looked away.

After that, things happened fast. Sheriff Justin and the prosecuting attorney entered from the back and took their places. Seconds later the bailiff shouted, "All rise!" and Judge Evelyn Dickinson swept into the room. Middle-aged and petite, the judge settled her black robe into her elevated chair, assessed the assemblage with a sober glance, and declared the hearing begun.

Drew had kept in touch with Sheriff Justin and had told Chantalene what to expect. Martha's confession would be the only evidence presented today. The sheriff took the stand to verify the transcript of the confession already submitted to the judge.

Sheriff Justin told the court that in custody, with an attorney present, Martha had admitted organizing the two Bonds and Slim Jenks to hang Clyde Morrell because he'd raped Berta Bond and sexually abused Chantalene. The fact of Clyde's innocence, he said, deflected from her reasoning "like petals off a stone." In Martha's mind the characters of Clyde and her own father were fused inseparably.

"She further admitted murdering LaVita Morrell to keep her from reclaiming her daughter," the sheriff said, his voice flat and emotionless. "She said a higher power had put the girl under her protection."

Chantalene looked at the back of Martha's brown-and-gray streaked hair, frizzing out behind her shoulders. The slight nodding of her head, as if she were agreeing with a sermon at the Baptist church, made Chantalene's stomach roll.

Sheriff Justin summarized the rest. Big Willie Bond had attempted unsuccessfully to extort money from Martha. When he threatened to kill Chantalene, Martha picked up the meat saw and silenced him forever. She also related—with great compassion, according to Sheriff Justin—Slim Jenks' attack of conscience for taking part in the hanging, and how she'd kept him dosed with tranquilizers to help him sleep.

"Which no doubt added to his depression," Drew whispered.

Martha's lawyer entered a plea of "not guilty by reason of insanity" and Judge Dickinson bound her over for trial. Drew had predicted the plea, but also told Chantalene he didn't envy Martha's attorney's job of selling it to a jury. "I'll bet he can't find a single witness who's seen Martha commit one irrational act in the last forty years," he'd said.

*Except for me,* Chantalene thought.

The judge remanded Martha for a thirty-day psychiatric evaluation before setting a trial date. Abruptly as it had started, the hearing was over.

Chantalene sat motionless while Martha was lead away and the spectators filed out of the courtroom. She felt strangely let down. She'd come to court expecting some kind of closure, but the legal process seemed too formal and bloodless to mark the end of anything.

Drew gathered her crutches. "Ready to go?"

Outdoors, Thelma Patterson was waiting for them on the steps, looking like a plump pillar of flowers. Chantalene didn't feel like hearing Thelma's repertoire of gossip today, but at least the postmistress was never malicious, only nosy.

"I heard Opal Bond admitted delivering that chicken's head to your doorstep," Thelma said, her eyes sparkling. "But she still swears she knew nothing about Willie and Willie being in on the lynching."

When Chantalene didn't respond, Drew held up the other end of the conversation. "Little Willie confirmed that, but I still think she must have known."

"You think he's lying to protect his mother?" Thelma asked.

Drew smirked. "I think he'd rather lie than tell the truth on any given subject. He's still denying his part in the lynching. But even if they brought charges against Opal, she'd probably get off with a battered-wife defense."

"She's put the farm up for sale," Thelma reported. "Gonna buy her a little house in El Rio close to the county home where Berta is."

Thelma leaned closer. "I've got something in my car for you, Chantalene." Her dark eyes danced. "Something valuable."

Chantalene couldn't imagine what Thelma would value more than the gossip she'd already shared. "Is that right?"

Thelma smiled, drawing out the suspense. "I'm going over to the Brass Kettle for early lunch. Why don't you kids let me buy you the best chicken fried steak you ever set your teeth on?"

Chantalene's stomach shuddered, but she didn't feel ready to drive back to her isolated house. She raised her eyebrows to Drew, thinking the invitation might appeal to his carnivorous appetite.

His forehead wrinkled when he met her eyes. "Why don't you go? I'd like to dig through those old records at the sheriff's office while I'm in town. I could meet you at the restaurant in an hour."

She nodded, knowing his purpose. She'd have preferred to go with him, but he needed time and space to exorcise his own ghosts.

How long had it been since she'd eaten in a restaurant? The Brass Kettle was pleasant and sunny and Chantalene relaxed against the vinyl seat. She pictured her future as a normal person, doing the simple, everyday things other people did. Already her nightmares were receding. Last night she'd slept straight through, with only one memorable dream that featured Drew and a king-sized waterbed. She wouldn't mind at all if that one recurred.

She ordered a chef's salad and homemade coconut pie. Thelma didn't mention the "something valuable" again, and Chantalene didn't ask. She felt oddly patient, willing to let events unfold instead of prying them loose. The change made her smile.

Thelma's chicken-fried steak covered all but the rim of a blue willow plate. She'd eaten only half of it when Drew joined them. He ordered the chicken fry as well, teasing Thelma about the calories while flattering her in his conversational way. But Chantalene noticed traces of tension around his eyes and the resigned droop of his shoulders. She didn't ask. He'd tell her when he was ready.

The pie was to die for. High on sugar, her patience gave way to curiosity. Besides, she knew Thelma was waiting for her to ask.

"Okay, enough stalling. What valuable something do you

have in your car for me?" She smiled, a willing participant in the game.

Thelma rounded up the last bite of steak on her plate and popped it into her mouth, chewing a few strokes before she answered. "Slim Jenks' violin."

Chantalene's napkin stopped halfway to her mouth. She'd forgotten all about Slim's last act of contrition.

Thelma's eyes glittered. "The label inside says it's a Landolfi. The lady at the music store here in El Rio says that if it's certified as an original, it might sell at auction for as much as fifty thousand dollars."

On the street outside the Brass Kettle, Thelma unlocked her car and moved a crocheted afghan from the floor in back. Underneath it lay a curved leather case, darkened with age. Thelma placed it in Chantalene's arms like a baby.

"Monkey asked me to give it to you," Thelma said. "He didn't think you'd want to see him."

Chantalene held the case awkwardly. "I can't take this."

"Yes, you can," Thelma said gently. "Monkey wants you to have it. He said it might pay your land out of debt."

Tiny cracks etched the curved edges of the case like antique porcelain. Chantalene thought of her visit with Slim Jenks the night before he died and swallowed a tightness in her throat.

"Monkey has acknowledged Slim's hand-written letter as his last will and testament," Drew said. "The violin belongs to you, legally."

*Get my farm out of debt ... or get far away from Tetumka,* she thought, looking up at Drew. *Maybe as far as New York.*

# TWENTY THREE

A crisp north wind swept among the headstones of Tetumka Cemetery. Autumn had come at last. A row of cedar trees along the eastern boundary leaned in unison, like praying nuns. On a barbed wire fence that separated the graves from a furrowed wheat field, a meadowlark sang for LaVita Morrell's long-delayed funeral. Chantalene balanced on her crutches and watched Reverend Graves lower the sealed urn containing her mother's ashes into the earth next to her father, their remains together at last. Perhaps their spirits always had been.

Diamond-bright sunshine collected on the shoulders of her black coat and she closed her eyes to absorb its warmth. Her mother's face floated before her, laughing, her ebony hair wild as the wind. From now on, she'd hold that memory of LaVita.

Beside her, Drew stood with his hands clasped loosely in front of him, and across the gravesite Thelma Patterson bowed her head. Five mourners for her mother, counting the meadowlark.

Oddly, Chantalene missed the comforting, bulky presence of Monkey Jenks. She hadn't expected him to attend, of course. Still, he was the single steadying force in her life for many years, and she felt certain that he hadn't known of Martha's plot until years after the fact. In a way, he too was a victim of Martha's madness, and she harbored no bitterness toward him. Other people might find that hard to understand, but they hadn't lived with Martha.

Drew helped the Reverend fill in LaVita's small grave, and Chantalene placed a bough of wild roses on the earth.

On their way out of the cemetery, she and Drew paused a few silent moments at the tombstone of Rose and Matt Sander.

Drew's face clouded. "Dad wasn't one of the vigilantes," he said, "but he wasn't innocent. The report said he found Clyde's body and called the sheriff, but he either told Sheriff Justin he cut Clyde down or let him assume it. When in fact, he must have found his body on the floor where you and your mother left him." His voice tightened. "Dad had to have deduced what really happened in his barn. But he kept quiet, or helped cover it up, so the official conclusion would be suicide."

She had suspected as much. "Don't judge him," she said quietly. "He had a tough decision and chose not to rat out his neighbors. Most people in his situation probably would have done the same."

A muscle twitched in Drew's jaw. "I guess I expected Dad to have more character than *most people,*" he said. "But he never did have much respect for the law."

He lifted his gaze to the fields beyond. "The worst is, I've followed his example. Some of the things I've done for my father-in-law's company ... I know it's dishonest, even when I find legal loopholes to protect him. I've violated my attorney's oath in a hundred petty ways."

She leaned against him for a moment. Drew squeezed her shoulder, and they walked back to his car. The wind stirred a cottonwood near the fence line and yellow leaves rained down on them as they drove away.

When he stopped the car in front of her house, he left the motor running.

"Come in?" she said.

"Can't," he said, and smiled. "I have cooking to do." He had promised her dinner in his newly remodeled kitchen. "Pick you up at six-thirty."

She met him at the front door that evening wearing a tiered black skirt that hid most of her cast, although the bulge made one hip look bigger than the other. She'd coerced her hair into a French braid, but frizzy spirals escaped around her face. She wore no jewelry at the scooped neck of her red blouse, only the gold hoop earrings that had been her mother's.

"Wow," Drew said.

She smiled. "Thank you very much."

He closed the door and shoved his hands in his pockets while she negotiated the porch steps with Bones leaping dangerously in front of her.

"Stop cringing," she chided.

"I'm doing my best."

She'd read him her rights more than once when he kept trying to take care of her.

He drove slowly, with the car windows open to the fall-scented air and his hand over hers on the seat. A warmth that was beginning to feel familiar curled up her arm and settled behind her breastbone, a heady sensation that felt both safe and dangerous.

"So is this our first official date?" she asked.

"I hope so."

He lifted her hand, turning it over, and kissed her palm. The gesture stopped her breath. She turned her eyes quickly back to the road, cupping the promise in her hand.

Though Drew had visited her daily since she'd broken her leg, she hadn't been to his house for several weeks.

When he turned the Volvo into the driveway, it was her turn to exclaim.

"Wow!"

His smile looked boyish and proud. "The old place is shaping up, isn't it? I could hardly wait for you to see it."

He had painted the trim a putty color that would blend with brick now stacked in the front yard. "Next week, the brick masons will face the house half-way up and build a chimney for an old-fashioned wood-burning stove," Drew said.

"All this just to sell the house?" An uneasy suspicion wrinkled through her mind, but Drew only shrugged and ushered her inside.

The refinished hardwood floor in the living/dining area shone rich and warm, and he'd laid a Mexican tile entryway. With no furniture, the room looked huge, especially compared to her small place.

"Wait till you see the kitchen. I should warn you, though, that a modern kitchen didn't turn me into a good cook," he said.

She sniffed. "I smell garlic and tomato sauce. It can't be bad."

They sat in the kitchen on two wooden chairs he'd found in the attic. For a table, he'd placed plywood across sawhorses and covered it with a folded bed sheet. A brown beer bottle, sans label, held sprigs of wild honeysuckle.

"This is marvelous!" She laughed, truly delighted.

He opened a bottle of wine and served a bachelor version of pasta primavera. "The best paper plates money can buy," he joked. But he'd bought two crystal glasses for the occasion.

"I'm celebrating tonight," he told her, lifting his glass. "I got a letter from Emily's lawyer, and she's accepted my settlement offer. I'm practically single, if not unencumbered."

The warmth rose up again, and it had nothing to do with the wine. "Congratulations." She touched her glass to his and sipped. "So what's next?"

He shrugged. "It takes a few weeks to become final."

"No. I mean, will you be going back to New York soon?"

He met her eyes. "I quit my job."

"Really!" The news shouldn't have surprised her, but it set off another ripple of foreboding. "So what will you do?"

"I can liquidate some mutual funds to get by for a while. Actually, I've been approached by a couple of the local folks about doing legal work for them." He smiled. "Thelma wants me to get her long-lost husband declared legally dead."

Chantalene raised her eyebrows. "Do you suppose Billy Ray's going to have a successor?" She smiled at the thought.

"If so, it may be the first secret Thelma's ever kept." He rolled the wine inside his glass and watched it thoughtfully. "I'm thinking of hanging out a shingle. I'd have to get licensed in Oklahoma first, of course."

"You're going to *stay* in Tetumka?" A vision of herself and Drew among the bright lights of New York evaporated like a mirage. She'd known all along the idea was foolish, but couldn't help regretting its loss.

He shrugged. "Where else would I go? At least I have a roof over my head."

She eyed him sharply. "That's not the whole reason and you know it. You love this farm. This land."

He examined his wine glass again. "I guess you're right. Six weeks ago I'd never have believed it, but I'd like to farm my own land. At least try it for a couple seasons." He met her eyes again. "But the land isn't the only thing keeping me here."

Her conflicted emotions must have shown. His face flushed as if he'd been rebuffed. "I can see you're thoroughly charmed by that confession."

She squirmed, regretting the moment she'd spoiled. "Actually, I *am*," she said.

"But?"

"But I've been thinking how much I'd like to get away from Tetumka. Maybe live in a big city somewhere. Get a job where I can use my computer skills and live above subsistence level. Finish college, eventually."

He paused. "I see."

"I have a lot of bad memories here. The whole town would be happier with me gone. Besides, I won't be able to work my truck farm next spring. This cast stays on six months minimum, they tell me." She grimaced. "I don't know how I'll stand it."

Drew slumped in his chair. "It's natural that you want to get out of Tetumka. You're only twenty-four, after all. You need to see something of the world." His voice sounded heavy.

"Twenty-five. I had a birthday last month."

"Why didn't you tell me?"

"I was sort of busy."

He set his glass on the table and pushed his plate away. "Suddenly I feel like an old man."

She turned her hand over on the table, remembering the heat she'd held in her palm. The future seemed distant and ambiguous. Right now, she was certain of only one thing she wanted.

"Of course," she said, drawing the words out slowly, "I can't very well move anywhere until my leg heals. Meanwhile, I'll have spent Slim's legacy getting out of debt, and I'll need a job."

He glanced up.

She tilted her wine glass at a careless angle. "Do you know anybody who needs a good legal assistant?"

A smile began at the corners of his mouth and spread to his eyes. "What are your qualifications?"

She placed her arms on the table and leaned her shoulders forward, watching his eyes flicker to the neckline of her blouse. She saw his youth returning.

"I have a natural talent for research and I'm a whiz at word processing." She raised her eyebrows and lowered her voice. "Plus a few other astonishing skills never before practiced on a New York lawyer."

His smile turned carnal as he picked up the wine bottle and refilled their glasses. "I doubt *that.* We big city lawyers have seen it all."

"Wanna bet?"

"I hope you're prepared to prove such a rash claim."

*"No problem."* He had no idea.

A hip-to-toe leg cast makes life more difficult, she thought later, but anything's possible if you're creative and determined.

No problem.

*About the Author*

M. K. Preston grew up on a wheat farm in Oklahoma, near a town not too different from the setting of her mystery series. Preston still lives in central Oklahoma where the rivers run red in Springtime and the cottonwoods lean toward the North Star. By day she edits and publishes *ByLine,* a nationally distributed trade magazine for writers.